"Satisfying me won't be easy."

A slow, knee-weakening smile curved his lips.

There went those butterflies in her belly again. Liz knew from experience what a passionate, generous, tireless lover he'd been as a teenager. She could only imagine how experience and patience had improved him. They'd fit perfectly together, their limbs tangled, melting from pleasure.

Sawyer was the only man to ever give her butterflies. Let alone with just a smile.

With their lips a hairsbreadth apart, she couldn't help but wonder if he tasted the same.

She tried to check any emotion from showing on her face, not letting him see how much his proximity or his words or his smile affected her. "Like I said, I can handle anything."

"We'll see." He stepped aside. "Let's go catch a killer."

WYOMING MOUNTAIN INVESTIGATION

JUNO RUSHDAN

INTRIGUE

For all the survivors of tragedy who never lost faith or hope.

ISBN-13: 978-1-335-45679-3

Wyoming Mountain Investigation

Copyright © 2024 by Juno Rushdan

Recycling programs for this product may not exist in your area.

For questions and comments about the quality of this book, please contact us at CustomerService@Harlequin.com.

Harlequin Enterprises ULC
22 Adelaide St. West, 41st Floor
Toronto, Ontario M5H 4E3, Canada
www.Harlequin.com

Printed in Lithuania

MIX
Paper | Supporting responsible forestry
FSC® C021394

Juno Rushdan is a veteran US Air Force intelligence officer and award-winning author. Her books are action-packed and fast-paced. Critics from *Kirkus Reviews* and *Library Journal* have called her work "heart-pounding James Bond-ian adventure" that "will captivate lovers of romantic thrillers." For a free book, visit her website: www.junorushdan.com.

Books by Juno Rushdan

Harlequin Intrigue

Cowboy State Lawmen: Duty and Honor

Wyoming Mountain Investigation

Cowboy State Lawmen

Wyoming Winter Rescue
Wyoming Christmas Stalker
Wyoming Mountain Hostage
Wyoming Mountain Murder
Wyoming Cowboy Undercover
Wyoming Mountain Cold Case

Fugitive Heroes: Topaz Unit

Rogue Christmas Operation
Alaskan Christmas Escape
Disavowed in Wyoming
An Operative's Last Stand

Visit the Author Profile page at Harlequin.com.

CAST OF CHARACTERS

Liz Kelley—Once the victim of a tragic fire, she rebuilt her life despite the scars she still carries. As an FBI agent, specializing in arson and bombings, her priority is seeing justice served. Her worst nightmare is going back home, but she has no choice in order to stop a killer.

Sawyer Powell—Arson investigator. He's haunted by the fire that changed both his and Liz's lives forever, destroying the future they had dreamed of together. Fifteen years later, he can't forget Liz or let go of the love he has for her.

Ted Rapke—Laramie Fire Department chief.

Erica Egan—This journalist will cross any line for a scoop and to see her name in the byline.

Holden Powell—Chief deputy sheriff and Sawyer's supportive brother.

Ashley Russo—A dedicated deputy in the sheriff's department.

Prologue

Wild Horse Ranch
Located between Laramie and Bison Ridge, Wyoming
July 3
Fifteen years earlier

Sprinting as fast as possible, lungs burning, he ran full-out from the clearing into the dark forest to be sure no one saw him. Once well in the woods, he stopped and leaned against a tree. Heart pounding, he caught his breath.

Beneath black clothes, he sweated from exertion. From the sweltering July night despite the strong breeze. From anticipation pumping in his veins. From fear that his plan might not work.

Come on. It should be an inferno by now. What was taking so long?

Another full minute ticked by. The big house should've gone up like dry kindling.

What had he done wrong? Did he need more accelerant? Should he go back to check?

Patience. Just wait.

Looking past the horse stable and two cabins of sleeping teens, he stared at the main house on the hill where Dave and Mabel Durbin lived. He'd made sure no one could help the unsuspecting Durbins. First, he'd locked the doors of the summer camp cabins and then the bunkhouse that was located far behind the stable. The barracks-like building was full of men who worked on the ranch.

Sweat dripped down his face and body, collecting everywhere on his skin. He clenched his jaw, his breath still coming hard from his chest, his nerves strung tight.

A gust of wind whipped through the dry leaves, rattling the brittle branches of the trees overhead. On the hill, smoke rose in the air, the smell filling his nose. Finally, the fire was taking hold. Flames burst to life on the house with a crackle that swelled to a roar. Like a supernatural monster, crimson and gold, it clawed and crawled its way up the sides of the house.

More perspiration rolled down his face, stinging his eyes. He lifted his mask and wiped his face with a gloved hand, but caution had him pull it back down *just in case*.

The fire blazed bright now, pulsing with hunger, growing bigger and hotter, spreading across the roof. He stared with grim satisfaction.

So beautiful. Powerful. Hypnotic against the pitch-black sky.

His creation. He'd been the one to give it life and set it loose.

A sudden gust of dry wind, bearing hard from the north, swept over the house, fanning the flames. Carrying sparks on the breeze to nearby trees. Glowing embers rained from the branches, falling on the two cabins. It wasn't long until the timbers of both roofs caught fire. The flames swirled and swelled, slithering down the walls, burning faster than he imagined possible. Much faster than the main house.

This wasn't part of his plan. A few of those sleeping teens trapped inside were innocent. The rest he blamed even more than the Durbins. He'd intended to make them suffer, too, once they were older and had more to lose than just their lives.

Fate was intervening, making it happen sooner rather than later. In a way they were all to blame. Guilt by association. The fire would make them pay. Without remorse. Without mercy. It would punish those responsible. This was sweet vengeance.

After tonight, the summer camp on the ranch would close forever.

He smiled, excitement bubbling in his chest. Watching the flames do what was necessary, he was enthralled. No. He was in love. This was the best high of his life. Better than playing football and scoring touchdowns. Better than sex.

If only he'd known what a thrill this would be, he would've done it sooner. For Timothy…and for Birdie.

There weren't any screams yet. The cabins weren't up to code and didn't have smoke detectors. No alarms to wake them. Maybe the smoke would kill them in their sleep before the flames. Not quite the punishment or death he'd wanted for them. They deserved much worse.

Twigs snapped, hurried footsteps trampling the earth. He spun in the direction of movement—to his left in the woods. Two figures raced toward the clearing.

No!

A teenage girl darted from the tree line first, her long hair flowing in waves under the moonlight. Lean, pale limbs pumped hard in panic.

Liz. She worked at the camp and was on his little hit list. Why wasn't she locked in the girls' cabin with the others?

The answer burst from the woods, not far behind her. Sawyer Powell. Her stinking boyfriend. He wasn't a camper or a worker and had no business being there.

Sawyer was like his self-righteous brother, Holden. The

former was the star of the basketball team, the latter was the quarterback. Golden boys who thought they walked on water at high school. Did whatever they wanted. Of course, he'd break the rules by being here.

"I'm calling 911." Liz was dialing as she ran.

No, no. Liz and Sawyer, a pair of meddlers, getting in the way. The dude ranch was smack-dab between both towns. One of the fire departments might get there in time.

Liz bolted to the double doors at the front of the girls' cabin and yanked on them. "I can't get it open! They've been tied shut!"

Although he'd made knots that would be hard to undo, in hindsight, chains and padlocks would've been smarter than using ropes.

"Break a window!" Sawyer grabbed a rock and shattered a windowpane, smashing around the frame. The lanky guy hopped up, disappearing inside the boys' cabin.

Liz did the same, scrambling into the other cabin. Those two were ruining everything.

Fists clenched, every sense alive, he gritted his teeth. This was not how it was supposed to end, with Liz Kelley and Sawyer Powell being heroes.

Teens dressed in pajamas funneled out through the broken windows, jumping onto the grass. Coughing and gagging, they backed away from the cabins. Some of them hurried up the hill toward the main house, shouting for the Durbins and yelling for help.

Liz and Sawyer might have stopped his plan, but they wouldn't stop him.

Everyone involved with what happened to Timothy would either burn or wished they had after he was finished with them. All the people who'd remained silent. Those who had looked the other way. Those dirty souls who benefited.

He saw their faces. Knew their names. Not only the ones on the ranch tonight. There were others and there would be justice. He would light their world on fire and burn it to the ground. One day. No matter how long he had to wait.

Liz emerged from the fiery cabin with the last girl. They backed away from the flames as Sawyer climbed out the boys' cabin window. Dropping to the ground, he gulped in air. Liz turned away from the cabins. Her jaw dropped and she took off.

He pivoted to see where she was going. The horse stable was burning, too! The wind was spreading the fire with blistering speed, feeding it fast, making the thinner structure of the barn go up like tinder. Horror whooshed through him. Helpless animals weren't supposed to get hurt.

Liz threw open the doors and rushed into the stable. A moment later, horses darted from the barn, one at a time. Could she get the stalls open and save them all in time?

For a painful second, his heart squeezing in his chest, he contemplated helping the horses. But he'd be seen for certain. He would be caught.

Hacking on the ground, Sawyer glanced around. He stumbled to his feet. "Liz!"

"She's inside the stable!" a girl screamed, pointing at the building engulfed in flames, and Sawyer made a beeline for it.

Men busted through the door of the bunkhouse, storming outside and sprinting into action. Some ran toward the main house while the rest headed for the stable.

Horses were still being set free. Sawyer was almost there. Another horse charged out of the burning barn, but no sign of Liz. Fire shot out through the roof. Sawyer hesitated. Afraid.

With a thunderous crunch, the roof of the stable collapsed, sending sparks shooting into the air like a million mini flares.

Two men wrapped themselves in blankets. Others threw buckets of water on them. Then the men rushed into the stable.

Why bother? Could she have survived?

Doubtful. Even if she had, the chances were slim they'd get her out alive. The only thing that could save Liz now was luck.

Chapter One

Fifteen years later
Present day

Special Agent Liz Kelley made her way through the Denver International Airport, eager to get back to work at Quantico.

Her cell phone buzzed. She fished it out of her oversize laptop bag. Glancing at the caller ID, she groaned. "Hi, Mom," she said, forcing herself to sound upbeat.

"How was the law enforcement symposium, sweetheart?"

"Fine, I suppose, all things considered."

"I'm sure it was better than fine," her mom said, ever the optimist. "I bet you did fantastic."

Only if *fantastic* meant "regrettably stilted and anxious." Since she survived a tragic fire as a teenager, she preferred to stay in the shadows. She still carried scars from that night on the inside and out. Being in the spotlight, the sole focus of more than a hundred people for an hour, had been brutal. She'd choose taking down a serial bomber any day instead.

Reaching her gate, Liz took a seat far from the desk and most of the other passengers, sitting with her back to a wall. Scanning the area, always assessing whether any potential threats lurked, she parked her rolling carry-on beside her.

"Not really, Mom." She adjusted her scarf that covered the

puckers on her neck. In her profession, it was easy to hide the telltale signs of the numerous skin grafts and most of the remaining scars that ointments didn't smooth out with long sleeves, her shoulder-length hair and trademark neckerchiefs. "The only reason my boss chose me is because the book has gotten so much attention. Public speaking and teaching really aren't my forte."

"You have to stop downplaying your achievements, Liz. You wrote an insightful book, and you're one the FBI's top profilers working for a special task force."

"It's called the BAU," Liz said, referring to the Behavioral Analysis Unit, where she'd worked at Quantico for the past eighteen months. A series of tough cases and a track record of impressing her supervisors had earned her a coveted spot. "It's a specialist department, not a task force." They coordinated investigative and operational support functions, as well as criminological research to assist federal, state, local and foreign law enforcement agencies investigating unusual or repetitive violent crime.

"Anyway, my point is that you're exceptional, and the FBI recognizes it."

Shaking her head, Liz smiled at how her mother looked at her through rose-colored glasses. "It does take a certain type of person who thrives at getting into the minds of the sickest, darkest criminals out there. An achievement that I'm sure is hard for you to brag about during your quilt guild meetings or bridge club."

"They're not the right audience, but it's their loss. Your dad's hunting buddies think it's cool." Her mom's voice brightened with enthusiasm. "Sweetheart, I hope you appreciate how lucky you are."

Lucky Liz. That's what everyone in her hometown had called her after she had survived the fire on the dude ranch.

The one that had killed Dave and Mabel Durbin. Yet they'd always said it with a wince or such unbearable pity in their eyes that her parents decided to move from Bison Ridge, Wyoming, to Missoula, Montana, to give her a fresh start, where she could heal. Homeschooled for the remainder of high school. Gone were the days of wearing shorts and tank tops and running on the cross-country team. An end to nosy townsfolk and concerned friends dropping in uninvited, forcing a smile at the sight of her, with stares that lingered too long. No more whispers when they thought she couldn't hear them. *At least her face wasn't ruined. That's still pretty.*

Her parents had sold most of the land on their property to the Shooting Star Ranch next to them, owned by the Powells, but had kept the house, which had been in the family for generations. They hoped she, their only child, would want it someday.

As far as Liz was concerned, she never again wanted to set foot within a hundred miles of where she'd suffered and had lost so much. Too many painful reminders.

Even being in Denver was cutting it a bit close for her liking.

"Yeah, Mom, I know I'm fortunate." And she was. To be alive. To have a successful career where she got to make a difference and save people.

But the blazing inferno that summer had robbed her of beauty and the chance for a normal life at only seventeen years old. In its place, she had been given a need—an obsession—to understand the mind of someone like the arsonist responsible for changing her world forever.

None of it felt like the kind of luck that was good.

Her phone beeped. She glanced at the screen. It was Ross Cho, the special agent in charge of her subsection, BAU 1.

"Mom, I've got to go. It's work on the other line. My boss probably wants to hear all about the symposium as well."

"Okay. Love you."

"Love you, too. Give Dad a hug from me." Liz disconnected and answered the other call. "Kelley."

"Where are you?" SAC Cho asked, his tone curt.

Liz stiffened. "At the airport, sir. I managed to get a standby seat on an earlier flight back to Virginia." There was no need to stay for the entire symposium once she'd done her part.

"Glad I caught you before you boarded. There's a change of plan. We received an urgent request for assistance from a fire investigation office that find themselves under an accelerated timeline. There appears to be an arsonist who is rapidly escalating. He's struck four times in the past twelve days. Five dead so far, another hospitalized in critical condition and not likely to make it. The most recent fire was earlier today, around eight this morning. Based on how things have been spiraling, we extrapolated that it's likely there could be another incident within the next day or two."

This was perfect for her instead of being a show pony at a conference. She lived for this kind of case.

Standing, she hoisted the strap of her laptop bag on her shoulder and pulled up the handle of her rolling carry-on. She had everything she needed, including her field jacket—windbreaker with FBI identifier—and agency-issued Glock. "I'll change my flight. Where am I headed and who is my point of contact?"

"We've booked a rental car for you. Check your email for the reservation. Looks as though driving is faster. Should take you roughly two and a half hours to reach Laramie."

A chill ran through her veins as the breath stalled in her lungs.

Laramie.

Time froze, as if her brain had shut down.

"The deputy state fire marshal there made the request and will be your POC," SAC Cho said. "He'll meet you at the site of the latest incident. I forwarded the address to you along with his information. The name is Powell. Sawyer Powell."

Sawyer, her ex-boyfriend? He's a fire marshal?

She hadn't seen or spoken to him since she'd moved away. Not that he hadn't tried to stay in contact after she left, but it had been too hard for her. The sight of him over video chat, the sound of his voice on the phone, even his bittersweet emails—all cruel reminders of another thing that she had lost.

Her first love.

Quickly, she banished the resurrected demons from her mind and gathered her thoughts. "Why me, sir? Surely there's someone in the Denver field office who could take this."

"You're the best I have on arson and bombings. There's no one in the Denver office more qualified to handle this than you. Besides, you're from Laramie. Don't you want an all-expense-paid trip back home?"

It was the last thing she wanted, considering the emotional havoc it might wreak for her.

"I'm from the neighboring town, Bison Ridge," she said, needing to make the distinction for some odd reason.

"Regardless, you know the lay of the land and you're in the area, more or less. What are the odds, huh? I guess the stars have aligned in your favor, as luck would have it."

Yeah, just her brand of luck. *Bad.*

Her voice, when she spoke again, was a rasp. "I guess so."

"I thought you'd sound more enthusiastic about being assigned this case," SAC Cho said. "It's the type you'd beg me to give you, but I'm sensing otherwise right now. What am I missing here? Is this going to be a problem?"

Squeezing her eyes closed, she reminded herself of what

was most important, why she did this job. Her tragedy had led her to the FBI, to become a criminal profiler with this specialization. What most civilians didn't understand, the part that wasn't shown on TV or covered in the newspaper was the long-term impact of arson. What it did not only to property but also to people, to families, to neighborhoods, to businesses. How it could destroy a small town.

If she could prevent another fire and the loss of more lives, then she had to do everything in her power to try. No matter the personal cost.

Liz opened her eyes and headed toward the rental cars. "No, sir," she said, stripping any weakness or doubt from her voice. "This won't be a problem. Thank you for the opportunity."

"That's more like it." Papers shuffled across the line. "There's one more thing before you go," Cho said, no doubt saving the best part for last. "This is about to get national coverage. Powell can't dissuade the mayor any longer from talking about it live on a major network."

Her stomach cramped. "Does the mayor have any idea how dangerous it is to give that kind of media attention to the UNSUB?" she asked, referring to the unidentified suspect. It would most likely make matters worse, only encouraging further incidents.

"Powell also thinks it's unwise, but the mayor isn't listening to him. It's an election year, citizens are dying, and businesses are being burned to the ground. Doesn't look good. The politician wants to control the narrative." He sighed as though there were more. "Listen, you've closed every case you've been assigned. Your record is flawless. I need you at your best on this one. Do you understand what I'm saying?"

Failure wasn't an option and she wouldn't have it any other way. Even though she was going back home, where the worst thing in her life had happened, all she had to do was keep the past in the past. There was never any room for feelings on an assignment. This time, it was especially true.

"Yes, sir. I understand." Absolutely nothing would get in the way of doing her job.

ARSON. AGAIN.

In his gut, Sawyer Powell was certain of it. Soon enough he'd have the evidence to support his hunch. Wearing his full PPE—personal protection equipment—kit, he followed protocol, starting with the least burned areas and moved toward the most damaged ones. Firefighters worked around him, making the scene more chaotic than he would've preferred. The fire had been extinguished, but now they were conducting overhaul. The process of searching for and putting out any pockets of fire that remained hidden under the floor, the ceiling or in the walls was laborious, but a single cluster of embers could cause a rekindling.

Ideally, he'd examine the area before overhaul began to ensure important evidence wasn't lost or destroyed. The station didn't enjoy having him underfoot, either. Yet they were working in tandem since time was something neither he nor the fire department had.

Sawyer was under mounting pressure from the mayor while the station was operating with only a small crew. They barely had enough for their three shifts that worked forty-eight hours on duty and ninety-six hours off duty. In their small town, where most of the action came from wildfires, that wasn't a problem. Until now.

He slowly walked the perimeter of the charity thrift store, jotting down notes for his report and taking photographs like an archaeologist mapping out a ruin. The air smelled of burned rubber and melted wires. Damp ash covered the floor, sticking to his boots.

Fire was a predictable beast. It breathed. It consumed. More importantly, it also spoke, telling a story. Sawyer only had to interpret. One thing he loved about his job was that fire didn't lie. Whatever it showed him would be the truth.

He picked up a large piece of glass from one of the broken windows. On it was a revealing spiderweb-like design. *Crazed glass.* A key indicator that a fire had burned fast and hot, fueled by a liquid accelerant, causing the glass to fracture.

He pushed deeper into the two-thousand-square-foot building. Ducking under insulation and wiring that hung down from the exposed ceiling, he came to the front of the office, where the victim who was now in the ICU fighting for her life had been discovered. Two firefighters inside had already opened up the walls and were getting ready to pull the lathe in the ceiling.

"Hey, guys, stop!" Sawyer called out, and the two looked over at him. They weren't from the station, but he recognized them from the volunteer crew that were sometimes called in. Many of them he knew by name. Not these two. "What are you doing? I need to examine this area before you destroy any potential evidence."

"Oh, okay," one said. "The chief told us to clean out the whole room. Nobody wants the dreaded and embarrassing call back to the scene because of a rekindle."

Sawyer tamped down his rising anger. "Slow everything down and think about what you're doing. In fact, why don't you take a break until I'm done?"

"But we were called in to give some of the station guys a break," the other one said. "We're fresh and ready to help. What do you want us to work on?"

Sawyer didn't care as long as they got out of his way. "Go ask the chief."

The pair shrugged and vacated the area.

Exhaling a perturbed breath, Sawyer looked around. He cleared some of the torn-down gypsum board and noticed deep charring along the base of the walls. Gases became buoyant when heated. Flames naturally burned upward. But this fire had burned extremely low down.

Near the door inside the office, he moved the remnants of a chair out of the way. Peculiar char patterns shaped like puddles were on the floor underneath. The type produced by a flammable or combustible liquid that caused a fire to concentrate in those kinds of pockets, creating *pour patterns*. What made the char strange was the intensity of the fire.

The same markings had been at the other two crime scenes along with something else. He removed more debris, sifting through ashes until he found it. Remnants of a mechanical device. He collected it, along with some of the surrounding rubble.

He snapped pictures and took samples to send to the crime lab. The bad news was it'd take several weeks to get the results. He glanced up at the ceiling and smiled. The good news was the clues the substance left behind pointed to gasoline as the accelerant. It burned downward, producing a hole exactly like the one at the center of the pour pattern on the floor. Then there was the highly volatile air and vapor mixture that always formed above burning gasoline, rising to the ceiling where it would ignite. He took photos of the severe ceiling damage over the spot.

Searching for any other similar burn patterns throughout the building, Sawyer identified a total of three points of origin. A fire had been set not only in the office but also by the rear and front doors. No doubt the fire had been intentionally set, creating a barrier to prevent the victim from escaping and from help easily reaching her.

The sadistic perpetrator had set a death trap. Disgust welled in Sawyer.

Stepping outside the building with the samples and his camera in the toolbox, he winced at the size of the crowd that had gathered nearby, a combination of civilians and reporters. It had doubled since he'd arrived.

Sawyer spotted Fire Chief Ted Rapke speaking to the two volunteers who had almost messed up the scene. He braced himself in expectation of the conversation that was to come.

They never got along when they worked side by side as firefighters, and after Ted was promoted to chief while Sawyer became the new fire marshal, instead of Ted's close friend, Gareth, things only got worse.

Ted raised a hand in Sawyer's direction and headed over to him. "There must have been some miscommunication, but there was no need for you to snap at those guys. Unlike us, they don't get paid to be out here. They freely volunteer their efforts as a way of serving and giving back to the community. I can't afford to lose them while some firebug is torching the city, killing people."

Sawyer pulled off his helmet and tucked it under his arm, aching to remove the rest of his gear in the sweltering ninety-degree August heat. "And I can't afford to have them tearing up valuable evidence if we're going to have any chance of catching whoever is doing this. Look, I get that your people are getting hammered."

"Try completely overwhelmed. I won't have you scaring off essential volunteers."

"That wasn't my intent." Sawyer took a breath, not wanting to utter the words on the tip of his tongue, but it couldn't be avoided any longer. "Overhaul is strenuous. The firefighters involved in suppression may be so fatigued afterward that they overlook hazards, along with evidence. As for the volunteers, they're not focused on preserving the scene so I can do my job. Their only concern is to help put out a fire and prevent a rekindling. Perhaps you should consider sticking to thermal imaging until after I've investigated and you can get a fresh crew for overhaul."

Ted folded his arms across his chest and narrowed his eyes. "Did you have the audacity to try and tell me how to do my job?"

"It was only a suggestion." One given to help them both be more effective.

"That takes some nerve, buddy," Ted said, "after Mayor Schroeder just got on national television and basically called you incompetent."

Clenching his jaw, Sawyer didn't even want to get started about the *mayor*.

Someone cleared a throat behind him. "Excuse me, gentlemen," a woman said, the voice familiar.

Sawyer pivoted, facing Liz Kelley, and the world dropped out from under him. Special Agent Cho had told him she was coming. Part of him refused to believe it until he saw her himself. The mention of her name alone had sent his pulse racing with anticipation.

Now, here she was standing in front of him. Her pale green eyes met his and he took in the sight of her. Same long wavy light brown hair. Same rose-colored lips. Trim figure albeit less gangly and curvier. A decade and a half older, and she still took his breath away.

"Oh yeah," Ted said. "Forgot to mention an FBI agent is out here waiting to do *your job* since you're having so much trouble on your own." The chief stalked off.

Ignoring Ted and their typical friction, Sawyer didn't take

his gaze off her. "Liz." He stepped in to hug her as she extended a hand to shake his instead. In the awkwardness, they both backed away, not touching each other at all. "Have you been here long?"

"Only a few minutes. The chief told me you were inside."

"It's good to see you. I only wish it was under better circumstances." Unease—the same he'd carried since Liz ended any contact—churned through him. All he wanted was to close the distance between them and be free of it. They'd once been inseparable, sharing everything, including a vision of the future. He missed that. Missed her.

She adjusted the scarf around her neck, pulling it up a bit over her scars. "Me too."

"FBI. How do you like working for the bureau?"

"It's fine. Good to have a purpose." She walked around him and faced the ruined building. "Are you sure this one is also arson?" she asked, cutting straight to business.

He removed his gloves. "With the classic V, multiple points of origin, crazed glass and puddle configurations caused by an ignitable liquid hydrocarbon accelerant that has a high boiling point, my guess is gasoline. I'm one hundred percent positive," he said, confident she understood all the jargon after having read her impressive book on behavioral analysis of serial arsonists and bombers.

She studied him a moment. Did she doubt him?

"I can get you some gear and we can take a look inside together," he offered, and it occurred to him she might not be comfortable going into a building that had been on fire only hours ago. How foolish to even suggest it. Then again, he wasn't sure how to manage this situation. Walking through the aftermath of a fire was probably regular protocol for her, but still he said, "Sorry if you'd rather not go inside."

Taking another step back, she shook her head. "It won't

be necessary. You're the expert in determining the cause. I'm here to help you figure out who's behind this."

It was the reason she was finally back in Laramie. To see justice served. To stop a sadistic killer.

He understood the drive and respected her for it. If only he knew how to handle working this case with her and the total gut punch he felt every time he thought about her.

"Do you mind?" he asked, opening his coat, not wanting to endure the heat any longer.

"Go right ahead." She took his toolbox and helmet, giving him a hand.

He stripped off the heavy turnout gear, leaving his pants and boots and his navy blue T-shirt that read Wyoming State Fire Marshal on the back.

"What can you tell me about the latest victim?" she asked.

"Ermenegilda Martinez. Thirty-one years old. Married. No kids. She runs the Compassionate Hearts charity and is currently in the ICU. It doesn't look good."

"This place doesn't open until nine. Any idea why she was here so early in the morning?"

He shook his head. "I'm hoping her husband will be able to shed some light on that."

"Have you been able to find a link between the victims?"

"Nothing so far." A failure that ate away at him, keeping him up at night.

"I haven't had a chance to review the case file since I drove straight here. I'd like to walk through all the details with you."

The back of his neck tingled, and he got the sense someone was watching him. He scanned the crowd of gawking spectators.

Of course, he was being watched. Right along with everyone else working. Many of the people in town were friends and associates. Most he knew by sight if not by name. Only one high school served both Laramie and Bison Ridge. He'd gone to school with almost everyone around his age, who'd grown up here, and had played sports with at least half of those working in the department. Scanning the faces of those who'd gathered, no one stuck out as a stranger.

Still, he couldn't shake the prickle of warning, which was worrisome. "Let's go to my office," he suggested, "away from prying eyes. And we can go over everything there."

"All right."

"Where's your car?"

"About three blocks away," she said. "There was no place to park around here."

"My truck is closer. I'm over there." He gestured in a direction less than a block away. "I'll take you to your car and you can follow me."

They walked past the fire station ambulance parked off to the side and around the crowd-control barricade, avoiding the mass of spectators. Serial fires and murders were unusual in the small, quiet town, where neighbors looked out for one another, and were bound to draw a ton of macabre interest.

A woman darted from the cluster of onlookers, rushing straight for them. He gritted his teeth at the sight of her, wishing they had been able to sneak by.

"Excuse me, Fire Marshal Powell!" She held out a recorder as she caught up to them. "I'm Erica Egan from the *Laramie Gazette*."

"I know who you are." *A menace.* Sawyer picked up his step and Liz kept pace with him.

Egan drew closer, her arm brushing his. "I've been trying to pin you down about the fires."

"I'm aware." He'd been warned about her. She had a reputation for pinning down and cozying up to guys for an exclusive. Didn't even matter if they were married. Sawyer wasn't one to buy into distasteful gossip that could ruin someone's career, but he didn't care for Egan's brand of reporting. Pure sensationalism.

"Would you care to comment on the things Mayor Schroeder had to say about you and the fires on the *Morning Buzz*? Is it the reason the FBI is here?"

He glanced over at Liz's jacket, which conspicuously announced the presence of a special agent. "I didn't watch or read about the mayor's appearance because I've been too busy working." It made him wonder how Ted had so many colorful details.

His truck wasn't much farther ahead. In a minute, he could hop inside and dodge answering any more questions.

"I'll recap for you." Egan shoved the recorder closer to his face. "The mayor said, and I quote, 'Arson Investigator Sawyer Powell'—"

"Hang on. Can you be quiet a moment," Liz said, putting a hand on his forearm, forcing him to slow down. "Do you hear that?"

He was about to ask, *What?* but in the quiet, it became obvious. There was a faint clicking sound. Was it coming from his vehicle?

"Bomb!" Liz yelled.

In the next heartbeat, his silver truck exploded in a fiery burst of heat and searing light, the violent boom rattling him to his core.

Chapter Two

Liz threw up an arm to shield her face. The ear-shattering blast rocked the ground, propelling the rear of the truck into the air and slamming it back down. The punch of the explosion knocked them off their feet as Sawyer wrapped his arms around her and the reporter.

Breath left Liz in a whoosh, pain shooting through her back when they landed hard on the pavement. Sawyer's sharp exhale rushed across her cheek. Her heart jumped into her throat.

A firestorm of blazing metal rained onto the street and over other vehicles. Liz was stunned, shaken but needed to get her bearings. Needed to move.

Get up. Get up!

She rolled Sawyer off her and started to sit up. A second explosion sent one of the truck doors whizzing through the air, flames erupting out the windows. Sawyer was back on top of her, protecting her with his body as fragments of glass and shrapnel sliced into the storefront sign beside them.

The smell of melting rubber and burning gasoline filled her nose. Her ears rang. Her eyes stung.

Liz pulled in deep breaths, trying to shake off her daze. Sawyer rolled onto his back with a groan.

She glanced to the right. "Are you okay?" she asked the reporter, who was lying face down with her hands covering her head. "Are you burned?"

"No. I don't think so." The woman whimpered. "Is it safe to move?"

"Yeah. I think so." Liz turned, checking on Sawyer.

Sitting up, he hissed in pain. She looked him over for injuries. There was a gash on his thigh and along the side of his torso where pieces of hot metal had scorched across his skin. His arm was pink, slightly singed.

"You're hurt." If only he had left his gear on or hadn't tried to shield her and the reporter from the eruption of fire and killing debris. She caressed his cheek, thankful it hadn't been worse.

"Oh my God." The reporter sat upright. "I—I can't believe what just happened."

Neither could Liz. Someone had tried to kill Sawyer and had nearly succeeded.

He fingered the rip in his trousers. "It's a clean cut." His gaze drifted to the pile of burning metal that used to be his truck.

"Can't say the same for your abdomen," Liz said, taking a closer look. A shard of metal was embedded in his flesh. "I'll get an EMT."

"No, I'll go." The reporter brushed off her clothes and slowly climbed to her feet. "It's the least I can do." A slight tremor rang in her voice. "You two saved my life."

Sawyer remained riveted on the wreckage. A bit of color had drained from his handsome face. Flames danced in his eyes. "A few feet closer, seconds really, and we would've been toast." He shook his head at the inferno that had been his truck.

Liz gingerly peeled up his shirt and looked at the wound. "It's bleeding pretty bad." But she didn't dare put any pressure on it with the piece of metal lodged in his side.

"I'll hurry." The reporter took off.

"Any chance you've upset someone that you know of?" Liz hiked her chin at the fireball.

"Enough to kill me?" He shook his head.

"Then whoever our suspect is did this."

"But why?" His voice dropped into a graveled tone.

Possibilities ran through her head. "They don't like the investigation. Maybe you're closer than you think to figuring this out. But the more important question is, why aren't we dead?"

Sawyer pulled his gaze from the flames and looked at her. "Come again."

"That bomb was planted with the intent to kill you."

"Maybe it was an aggressive tactic to scare me off."

She gave Sawyer a slow, noncommittal gesture with her head as she considered it. "Maybe." Although she doubted that was the case. "The bomb was big enough to set off a secondary blast," she said, thinking aloud. "That kind of explosion was meant to kill, not scare."

"Then why didn't he wait until we were in the vehicle to let it explode."

More possibilities rushed through her mind. "I can't say for sure, but I do know that it's one thing to kill a fire marshal and quite another if it's a federal agent," she said, and he grimaced. "No offense, but it's the difference between a state level and federal crime. Not to mention drawing the ire of the entire bureau by blowing up one of their own. The BAU would descend upon Laramie like the four horsemen of the apocalypse determined to bring the end of days to the perpetrator. Anyone smart would avoid that."

Smart enough not to let their agenda override common sense. She hoped her presence was the reason they hadn't been in the truck when it exploded. If it was something else, then this was bigger than she feared.

The ambulance pulled up. Sawyer tried to take the tool-box full of evidence with him, but Liz took it from his hands. She'd ensure it stayed in her possession or locked safely in her trunk.

Once the paramedics got him on a gurney and loaded into the back, she ran to her rental car and raced over to the emergency room at Laramie Hospital. After she flashed her badge, a nurse didn't hesitate to show her to the bay where they had put him.

Sawyer was lying on a bed propped up with pillows. She'd kept pictures of him, but all the photos were of him as a teen. Today was the first time she'd seen him as a man, and seeing his face after all this time was just short of ecstasy. His intense baby blue eyes met hers, a grin tugging the corner of his mouth, and her stomach fluttered. She drank in the sight of him. His sunny blond hair was too long in the front, still curly at the top in a way that had always made her want to run her fingers through it, and messier than before the explosion, but the rough-and-tumble look on him was appealing. His jaw squarer than she remembered and covered in stubble.

Pulling her gaze from him, she stepped inside the bay.

"A doctor will be in to see him shortly," the nurse said.

Liz gave her an appreciative smile. "Thank you."

The nurse left, drawing the curtain behind her, giving them some privacy.

"My personal hero returns," he said.

Liz shook her head. "I'm no such thing."

"All evidence to the contrary. You've been here less than an hour and already saved my life."

"I can't take credit for being a default deterrent." Possible deterrent anyway. The culprit deliberately triggered the bomb early, which had caused the clicking sound—something they wouldn't have heard until they were inside the truck if the intent had been to kill them. Clearly the person didn't mind taking lives, enjoyed it even, but was fear of committing a federal offense really the reason they were alive right now? Maybe if they were able to figure out the answer, it would help them find the killer. "How are you holding up?" Liz asked, going to his side.

"I'm alive, so I can't complain."

Well, he could, and she wouldn't blame him if he did. But the old Sawyer she knew never was one to complain or criticize and always the first to give a compliment. The best type of friend, who'd never let anyone down, especially not someone in trouble. Kind. Confident. Strong. In high school, he loved basketball, her, and numbers. He had talked about having a double major in college, business and finance. The perfect combination to become a quantitative analyst. A far cry from what he did today.

"How did you end up a fire marshal?" she wondered. "I thought you wanted to be a *quant*."

"I guess the same way you ended up an FBI agent." The humor bled from his tone as the light in his eyes dimmed.

Her dream of wanting to be a museum curator felt like something from a past life. In fact, it was distant enough to have been someone else's desire.

The tragedy that summer had altered the courses of their lives forever.

"I was a firefighter for a long time," he said, "until I realized I was better suited for going into the building after, piecing it together and figuring out the why."

Sawyer had always been a handsome hunk with picture-perfect looks, but she'd found his analytical mind even more attractive. It was good he was using it to help stop criminals instead of finding ways to make companies more profitable.

"Is there anyone I can call for you to let them know you're in the ER? Your wife? Girlfriend?"

Part of her hoped he had found happiness with another woman. A larger part wished he was unattached, which didn't add up in her head since she had been the one to cut him off. What he did with his life, the job he chose, who he loved, shouldn't matter, but in her heart, she'd clung to him. Out on a run, making dinner for one, in bed alone, in the stillness of the dark, he'd emerge like a phantom, haunting her.

"Nope. Not even a lover to complain when I work overtime," he said, and relief trickled through her. "I never got into anything serious, and anything fun tends to fade fast. More often than not, being with the wrong person is lonelier than being without them."

Something in his voice saddened her, too, making her regret her selfishness. He deserved to have the full life that she never would. "I'm surprised. You wanted to be married by twenty-five and have a couple of kids by now."

"After all this time, you still don't get it." His gaze narrowed on her as he cocked his head to the side. "That was *our* plan. The life I wanted with you."

His words sliced at her heart with the precision of a scalpel, but she didn't dare allow long-buried feelings to bleed through.

The bay curtain opened with a whoosh, thankfully diverting their attention.

"Hello," said a woman, entering as she stared at a medical tablet. "I'm Dr. Moreno." Her head popped up and she flashed a smile. "I hear you're not having a good day."

"You have no idea," Sawyer said.

Dr. Moreno set the tablet down and pulled on latex gloves. "Let's take a look."

"I'll step out," Liz said.

Sawyer put a hand on her forearm. "I'd prefer it if you stayed."

Dr. Moreno grabbed a pair of scissors and set it down on a tray. "He'll need a distraction in a moment."

"Then there's no one better than you, Liz," he said.

The doctor treated his leg first, cleaning the wound and applying a bandage. She slathered ointment on the pink area of his arm. Then she moved on to his abdomen and cut his T-shirt off, revealing his bare torso.

Warmth shot up Liz's neck, heating her face. He'd aged but hadn't changed for the worse in the past fifteen years. Somehow, he'd only gotten better looking. A few small lines etched the outer corners of his stunning eyes. He had quite a bit more bulk. The body of a teenage basketball player had been replaced with ridges and valleys of lean, sculpted muscle on a firefighter turned investigator.

He'd developed this body not only in the gym but the hard way. Hauling eighty pounds of gear and equipment up flights of stairs and into dangerous situations.

At least he no longer battled fires, but unless they found whoever planted a bomb in his truck, he'd be in danger.

"Okay, this next part is going to hurt." The doctor traded the scissors for forceps. She pressed down lightly around the wound and then gripped hold of the piece of shrapnel. As Dr. Moreno began extracting it, Sawyer grimaced. "Talk to him."

Liz took his hand in hers and squeezed. Thinking of something to say, anything to take his mind off the pain, she blurted the first thing to pop in her mind. "Hey, do you remember that time we went swimming, and afterward you surprised me with a picnic?" The lunch he'd packed had contained all her favorites.

He laughed. "Yep. I was the genius who laid out the blanket right under a hive of angry, territorial hornets. How could I forget?" He hissed when the doctor started the sutures.

Liz pressed her palm to his cheek, caressing his flawless skin with a thumb and drawing his full attention. "Right up until we got stung, the day had been perfect. Eighty degrees. Sunny. Warm breeze. Blue skies. Cool water. We swam and played around in the lake for goodness knows how long." He'd even brought an MP3 player. They'd danced and made out, and it had seemed like they'd have forever together. Kissing. Hugging. Dancing. Laughing. Holding each other close. "Another surprise—the tickets to the ballet in Cheyenne. *Swan Lake.*" He'd been an A-student and star athlete who also knew classical music and appreciated art—interests they'd shared. Everything she'd wanted in a life partner. "Nothing could've made the day better. Other than not getting stung."

There were no more perfect days. She hadn't even put on a bathing suit since…

"None of that is what made the day special." He tightened his fingers around hers. "It was perfect simply because we were together." The sincerity in his voice caused a pang in her chest.

"All done." The doctor removed her gloves with a snap of latex.

Liz slipped her hand from his. In her effort to distract him, she'd only sabotaged herself, rehashing beautiful memories she couldn't afford to dwell on. Every time she thought about Sawyer, what it was like to be with him, she softened.

It made her weak.

"The wound should heal in two to four weeks," Dr. Moreno said. "No arteries were cut, but I'm glad you didn't take the chance of removing the piece of metal. The stitches will dissolve on their own over time. I'll prescribe an antibiotic to prevent an infection and get you discharged. Take an over-the-counter analgesic for pain. Do you have any questions?"

"You have anything I could put on?" He gestured at his bare chest. "Other than a hospital gown."

"Sure. Plenty of scrubs around. I think we can rustle up a top for you."

"Thanks."

With a nod, she whipped back the curtain and disappeared.

"Liz." Sawyer reached for her.

But she stepped away from the bed. They needed to focus on finding a killer, not ancient history. "While we're here at the hospital, we should go up to the ICU. See Mrs. Martinez. Speak with her husband. We can go over everything else pertinent to the case afterward."

"Of course. Back to business. But we should also make time to talk. Clear the air. About us."

"There is no *us*," she said, almost as a reflex.

"You made sure of that by not returning any of my emails or phone calls. I get why you left Wyoming, but I never imagined you'd leave me, too."

They had been connected. The strongest bond she'd ever had, other than the one with her parents, but she'd acted in both their best interests.

"I went to Montana to see you once," he said, and her heart sank, not wanting old wounds to reopen. "Drove all night without sleeping. I need to know. Were you home that day when I knocked on the door?"

Of course she was there. After the move, it took her a year to leave the house. Her father had gotten rid of him without even asking her, which had been just as well since she'd hidden in the closet.

Like a coward.

"I would've sworn you were there," he said, "so I stood outside, calling for you."

The sound of him—screaming her name at the top of his lungs, pain racking his voice—had gutted her. The memory had tears stinging the back of her eyes.

"I was out there trying to remind you what you meant to me until I was hoarse and your dad called the cops."

No reminder was necessary. They'd practically grown up together, with their properties adjacent. Hers on the side of the Bison Ridge town line and his in Laramie. Since they were thirteen and first kissed, they'd been making plans.

Listening to him outside, she hid in the closet, grief-stricken over the end of her world as she'd known it, over the loss of the life they'd never have together. She forced herself to accept the reality that nothing would ever be the same again.

He'd needed to move on without guilt or any obligation to stay with her, the scarred girl who survived. And she had needed something he couldn't give her. To heal on her own. To build a new life. To do what felt impossible—reimagine her future without him.

It was the toughest decision she'd ever made, but she'd thought a clean break was best.

"Were you home?" he asked. "Just answer that much."

She had never lied to Sawyer. Not once. And she wouldn't start now.

Liz swallowed around the tight knot of guilt rising in her throat. "I'm not back in Wyoming for personal reasons," she said, telling him the one truth they needed to discuss at the moment. Emotions blurred lines, leading to mistakes, which endangered lives. After the bomb in his truck, one thing was certain. Failure could get them killed. She stiffened her spine along with her resolve. "I'm only here because of the case. It's all that matters right now."

SAWYER RODE IN the hospital elevator beside Liz, his chest aching. How could she think he'd be engaged, much less married with kids when he was stuck? His heart was trapped in limbo.

Not that she would know. She'd washed her hands of him without looking back and considering the impact of her choices on him.

He'd wished for a chance to talk to her face-to-face so many times, memorized the questions he'd ask, how she'd respond, wondering whether he'd finally get a sense of closure. None of his hopes included the two of them working a case together or her using it as an excuse to avoid having a long overdue conversation. Still, he clung to two little words: *Right now.*

He took that to mean eventually she would be willing to discuss what happened between them. Just not right now.

The pain he'd kept bottled up for a decade and a half—holding him prisoner to the past, unable to move on—would have to fester a while longer.

The doors opened to the ICU floor. He stepped off the elevator with his sole focus on the job.

They headed to the reception desk. "Hello. I'm Fire Marshal Powell," he said, pulling his badge from his pocket and flashing it at the nurse when she eyed his medical scrub top, "and this is Agent Kelley. We'd like to get an update on Mrs. Martinez."

"Her condition hasn't changed." The nurse's face tightened into a grave look. "She's on life support, but the extent of her injuries makes survival highly unlikely. The doctor thinks she has seventy-two hours at the most."

"Can you notify us if there's any change?" Liz asked, handing her a business card, and the nurse nodded. "What room is she in?"

"Three." She pointed to it. "Her husband is there with her. Only one person at a time is allowed inside."

"Thank you." This was the part of the job that sucked the most. Fire marshals had to pay these kinds of visits, too. Tell someone a loved one had died in a fire so severe their body was unrecognizable. Or ask them questions, probing into their life when they needed space to deal with their emotions. It was always hard on him.

They crossed the open space and stopped at the large window that provided the nurses with a view of the patient. Mr. Martinez sat in a chair beside the bed, his head bent, his hand resting near his wife's, wrapped in bandages, like her face, arms, and most of her body.

Her injuries were severe and extensive. Far worse than the condition Liz had been in. Sawyer had been by her side, too, giving her parents breaks, staying during the wee hours so they could go home, rest, shower and eat.

As close as he had been with Liz, their love strong and real, even for teenagers, he didn't presume to understand the magnitude of what Mr. Martinez must have been experiencing.

A thread of anger wove through Sawyer. They had to stop whoever was responsible before more lives were destroyed.

He glanced at Liz and saw the dark shadows swimming in her eyes. A slight shudder ran through her but only lasted a second. Anyone not carefully watching would've missed it. The sight of the latest victim fighting for her life in the ICU had to be hard on Liz, bringing awful memories to the forefront.

Once, when Sawyer was little, he was playing with one of his brothers, racing through the kitchen, and collided with his mom, who had been holding a pot of boiling water. The burn on his arm that formed had blistered and stung for a week. But his pain had been nothing in comparison to the agony Liz had endured.

Running into a burning building to save kids and horses took a singular kind of selflessness and courage. Her reward had been getting trapped under a burning beam that had fallen in the stables, flames melting her flesh and months of slow healing.

After suffering the unimaginable, she chose a career focused on arson and bombings. Faced what she must fear on a regular basis. She was remarkable.

Always had been.

"Are you all right?" he asked.

Her face was calm but her spine rigid. "I'm fine." The tight, clipped tone of her voice confirmed what he suspected despite her words.

She wasn't okay, but she was too strong to say otherwise.

Mr. Martinez looked up, catching sight of them. A burly man, he wiped tears from his eyes, stood in a weary way as though he might fall back into his chair and approached them.

They met him at the threshold.

"I'm Special Agent Kelley and this is Fire Marshal Powell. Can we speak with you for a moment regarding your wife?"

He nodded and she gestured for them to move over to a corner.

"Do you know who did this?" the husband asked.

"That's what we're trying to find out," Sawyer said.

Liz pulled a small notepad from her pocket. "What time does the Compassionate Hearts store open?"

"At ten. Every day."

"Any idea why she was there two hours early?" Liz asked.

Mr. Martinez sniffled. "To catch up on paperwork. She used to do it late at night, but I used to worry about her. Bad

things can happen late. I thought earlier in the day was safer."
A tear leaked from his eye.

"Generally speaking, it is," Liz said, taking notes. "Did anyone know she made a habit of coming in early?"

The husband shrugged. "Maybe some of the staff."

Sawyer thought back on how the fire had three points of origin and a theory he had. "When your wife went in early before the store opened, did she lock the door behind her or leave it open?"

"I can't say for sure, but I believe she locked it. Doris Neff worked mornings. She'd know."

"Do you have any idea why someone would have a reason to burn down the charity or harm your wife?" Liz asked. "Please try to think carefully about the smallest thing."

Mr. Martinez shook his head. "The thrift store gives all its revenue to help disabled veterans and impoverished children. Most of the people who work there are volunteers. As for my wife, she's the sweetest soul. No one would have any reason to hurt Aleida."

Sawyer exchanged a look with Liz before turning back to Mr. Martinez. "We thought her name was Ermenegilda."

"It is, an old family name but a mouthful. No one ever calls her that. Her grandmother went by Gilda. So, my wife uses her middle name. Aleida."

Liz tensed. "Neither are very common names. Thirty-one would put her at the right age. By any chance, is your wife Aleida Flores?"

"Yes, that's her maiden name. Do you know her?"

A strange look crossed Liz's face for a moment, and then it was gone, replaced by a stony expression. "I'm from around here. Bison Ridge, actually. I know a lot of people from there as well as Laramie. Thank you for your time. If you think of anything else, give me," she said, handing him a business card from her pocket, "or Fire Marshal Powell a call."

"The fire station can reach me if you dial their main office. We'll let you get back to your wife." They left the ICU. In the elevator, Sawyer waited until others got off and they were alone. "How do you know Aleida Flores?"

It was probably nothing, like she'd said. She knew lots of people, as did he, but something about her expression worried him.

"From the camp on the dude ranch," she said, her voice a whisper. "Aleida was there that night."

Everything inside him stilled. Silence fell like a curtain, the space around him becoming deafeningly quiet.

"One of the girls you rescued?" he finally clarified.

Staring straight ahead, her body stiff, Liz gave one slow nod. The strange expression came over her face again. She was probably thinking the same unsettling thing running through his head. Aleida had been saved from a deliberately set fire fifteen years ago only to be in critical condition with an unlikely chance of survival because of another one.

Coincidences happened every day, but this one he didn't like.

Chapter Three

Emotions seesawed through Liz. Seeing Mrs. Martinez had been harder than she had expected. While staring at the poor woman, for a heartbeat, Liz was trapped back in the burning stable, panic flooding her veins, frenzied horses, the crackling terror of the fire, the beam falling—pinning her, flames lashing her body, smoke clogging her lungs, searing pain.

Liz flinched. She often had terrible nightmares about that night, but this was the first time in over a decade that she had experienced a fresh wave of sheer fear while awake.

She couldn't help thinking back to her own time in the ICU, the mind-vibrating cacophony of the machines, the tubes, being in and out of consciousness while others whispered, thinking she couldn't hear. The shuddery breaths of her mother crying to her father. *Oh, honey, our little girl was perfect. Now I can barely look at her.*

Liz clenched her hands at her sides. Her internal wounds remained raw despite the time that had passed.

The elevator chimed and the doors opened. She shoved the horror of her personal tragedy into a far corner of her mind as they stepped out onto the first floor.

Another shiver ran through Liz. The shock from learning Aleida, the last girl she'd gotten out of a burning cabin and to safety, was Mrs. Martinez hadn't dissipated.

How could the universe be so twisted and cruel?

Or was there something else at play?

There was a saying that if you saved a life, you became responsible for it. Whether or not it was true, Liz didn't know, but she was more committed than ever to finding the monster who was setting the fires.

They had almost reached the doors to the parking lot when Erica Egan hopped up from a chair and made a beeline for them. The woman did not give up.

Liz hated the journalist's persistence as much as she admired it.

"You again?" Sawyer asked with a disgusted shake of his head.

The double doors opened with a whoosh.

Egan followed them outside. "I have a job to do, the same as you."

"Not quite the same," Sawyer said. "The more you stalk me, the more time you take away from me investigating."

The determined reporter hurried around to the front of them and raised her recorder. "Give me a quote. On the record," she said, but when Sawyer glared at her, she continued. "I just need something to work with. Anything. Come on."

"I've got a quote for you." Liz stepped close to the recorder. "Fire Marshal Sawyer Powell is doing an incredible job, getting closer to the truth each day. That's why he or she—but I'll stick with *he* since ninety percent of arsonists are white males from midteens to midthirties—targeted Powell today by planting a bomb in his truck that nearly took his life, as well as yours and mine."

Sawyer glanced at her with a quirked brow but didn't say a word.

"If that's true and he's doing such a good job, why is the FBI taking over the case?" Egan asked.

Liz folded her arms. "I'm not here to take over. I'm only here to assist. For a complex case such as this, usually an entire Behavioral Analysis Unit is required. Not one fire marshal working alone. Rather than being criticized, Sawyer Powell should be commended for having the foresight to reach out to the FBI."

The journalist cracked a smile.

"That's all for now," Sawyer said. "Egan, if you want to be part of the solution and not the problem, stop glorifying this pyromaniac who's murdering people. Less sensationalized prose about the fires in your articles that will only embolden him. Focus more on the innocent victims and the destruction of property, like a charity. This guy is a monster. Brand him as one and you'll get more quotes."

"Call me Erica." Shutting off the recorder, the pert reporter stepped closer to him, tilting her head as her features softened. Egan's face was classically beautiful. Platinum blond hair. Deep blue eyes. A svelte figure only a dead man wouldn't find attractive. "My writing style has boosted readership, which is what I was hired to do. I'm willing to consider what you've said, but not simply for more quotes. I want an exclusive. From you. We could discuss further over drinks. I'm buying."

Liz suddenly felt like she was intruding on something by simply standing there. Who was she to stand in the way of him having fun if that's what he wanted? "Sawyer, I'll wait for you over—"

"No need, Liz. Ms. Egan is the one leaving." He glanced back at the other woman. "I have no interest in having a drink with you, but if you reconsider your angle in future articles like I've asked, *we'll* give you an interview together when it's all over."

Egan's eyes went sly. "That could take weeks. How about a chat over coffee every morning?"

Liz swallowed a sigh, listening to this negotiation.

Sawyer glanced at her from the corner of his eyes, probably picking up on her irritation. "Once a week?" he countered.

"You don't expect to catch this guy soon, then." Egan flashed a slithery smile. "Every other day, locations to be determined by me."

A muscle ticked in Sawyer's jaw. "Fine," he said, wearily.

Triumph gleamed in the woman's eyes. "By the way," she said, turning to Liz, "what's your name? For my article."

"Special Agent Liz Kelley."

"The one who wrote the book?" Egan asked.

Liz was taken aback. "I'm surprised you've heard of it."

"You're famous around here. Sorry I didn't recognize you."

Was this town and Bison Ridge still talking about that tragic summer? About the *lucky* girl who survived?

Sawyer clasped her shoulder and squeezed. "It's not what you think," he said, his voice soothing. Their eyes met and recognition was written on his face about what was going through her head. "The Sage Bookshop had it in stock. Signed copies. Your mom even had a huge poster made with your picture on it. They hung it in the front window for months."

She remembered her mom had asked her to sign a bunch of copies, so she'd always have an autographed one on hand. Liz hadn't believed the far-fetched story, but she hadn't pushed for the truth, either. When it came to her mom, sometimes it was better not to ask.

The reporter's gaze landed on the spot where Sawyer touched Liz. "What's the history between you two?" Egan switched the recorder back on and held it up.

Sawyer dropped his hand as Liz backed away from him.

If only they could stop touching. "We're old friends. We used to be neighbors. Our properties are adjacent, but there are plenty of acres between us," Liz said, completely caught off guard, hearing herself babble. Not her style. Ever. She simply didn't want the past dredged up and rehashed on the pages of the *Gazette*.

She bit the inside of her lip to stop the verbal diarrhea.

"We're done here. Now, if you'll excuse us, we have work to do." Sawyer took Liz by the arm, cupping her elbow, and walked off.

Liz glanced over her shoulder. Egan watched them for a moment before she strutted off across the parking lot.

"At least you're going in the right direction," Liz said. "I don't recognize Egan. Is she from around here?"

"Moved here a couple of years ago."

Relieved the reporter was gone and hopeful Egan hadn't caught the whiff of a scoop, Liz took a deep breath. "There's my rental." She pointed out the sedan.

"Thanks for the quote." He let go of her arm. "You didn't have to say all that stuff about me."

"Yes, I did. Because it's true." Although she should've given her words deeper consideration rather than spouting off a knee-jerk quote. On the bright side, it was only a few lines in a local paper. Not a ten-minute tirade on a major national news network. "I heard what the mayor had to say about you on satellite radio during the drive. I don't know why Bill Schroeder is trying to hang you out to dry, but I won't stand for it."

She was acquainted with Bill well enough and had never cared for him. They were around the same age, with him being two years older, but Bill's entitled attitude rubbed her the wrong way. He was a bully back then and still was. Only this time he was using his position as mayor to pick on a civil servant who was trying to do his job.

"Voters are going to want to blame someone if I don't catch this guy."

"If *we* don't. You're not in this alone. Not anymore. We're going to nail this person. Together." Thinking back on Aleida in the ICU, Liz intended to see justice served.

"The one thing I miss about being a firefighter is working on a team. Being a fire marshal gets a little lonely." The corner of his mouth hiked up in a grin, his blues twinkling, making her stomach dip like she was seventeen years old again.

Shake it off, Liz.

She hit the key fob, unlocking the doors.

"Want to grab dinner over at Delgado's and go over the case?" he asked.

Eating at Delgado's with him, the way they used to, was an easy *no*. Too familiar. More nostalgia was the last thing she needed.

"I'm starving, but let's get it delivered to your office," she said. "There we can talk privately and openly, combing through the details while we wait for the food." She pulled on the handle, opening the door.

He put his hand on the top of the frame, blocking her from getting inside the car. "Did you mean what you said about us being a team?"

"Of course."

"Good, but it's going to require trust. The kind of trust where my life could be in your hands and vice versa. Until we get this guy, we're going to be joined at the hip. Can you handle all that?"

She wasn't the same petrified seventeen-year-old girl who hid in a closet because she didn't know how to stand on her own two feet after losing so much. "I can handle anything."

"Even if it's with me?" His gaze held hers, a clear challenge gleaming in his eyes.

He had no intention of putting the past behind them. He would keep pushing for answers, for the discussion that didn't take place in Montana all those years ago. The one she owed him.

She'd thought reliving the trauma of the fire would be the hardest part of coming back. Instead, the most difficult thing was blond, blue-eyed, six-three and two hundred pounds of pure stubbornness.

Time for her to go into damage control mode before he went on the offensive.

She drew closer, bringing them toe to toe. No more backing away from him, averting her gaze or acting like an awkward teenager scared of the slightest touch, giving him reason to doubt she could handle this—being "joined at the hip." Their familiarity could be a strength. They'd once been so in tune that they finished each other's sentences. They only had to find a new rhythm without letting the tempo get out of control.

"Even with you," she said. "I'll make you a deal. After we catch this guy, we'll sit down and talk." As much as she disliked scrapping her plan to hightail it out of town once the job was finished, it might be the only thing to appease him. "Really talk until you're satisfied. Okay?"

Leaning in, Sawyer brought his face dangerously close to hers, eliciting a different kind of shudder from her, but instead of retreating, she steeled her spine.

"Satisfying me won't be easy." A slow, knee-weakening smile curved his lips.

There went those stupid butterflies in her belly again. She knew from delicious experience what a passionate, generous, tireless lover he was as a teenager. She could only imagine how experience and patience had improved him. They'd fit perfectly together, their limbs tangled, melting from pleasure.

Not that she'd had other lovers to compare. She didn't even wear a T-shirt on a run, opting instead for a long sleeve, light-weight UV top. The idea of taking off all her clothes in front of a guy, the sight of her probably making his skin crawl, was unthinkable.

But Sawyer was the only man to ever give her butterflies. Let alone with just a smile.

With their lips a hairbreadth apart, she couldn't help but wonder if he tasted the same.

She tried to prevent any emotion showing on her face, not letting him see how much his proximity or his words or smile affected her. "Like I said, I can handle anything."

"We'll see." He stepped aside. "Let's go catch a killer."

Chapter Four

Closing the door to his office inside the fire station, Sawyer gestured for Liz to make herself at home.

"Have you been able to find any connection between the victims?" she asked, sitting on the sofa in the back of the room.

"None so far." Something he'd lost sleep over, wondering, why them?

"It would be good to have someone photograph the crowds at any other fires during the remainder of this investigation." Settling in, she removed her jacket but kept on the scarf, which, he now noticed, matched the color of her slacks.

Gunmetal blue. Custom-made.

Did she always wear a neckerchief around others? Or was she ever at ease in her own skin with someone else?

If so, he wanted nothing more than to be that someone. Still. Always.

"Do you think our suspect will be out there, again?" Sawyer sat behind his desk.

"It's highly likely. From the looks of what was left of the Compassionate Hearts building, he loves destructive fire. Roughly one-third of arsonists return to the scene. The primary attraction can be a desire for control and power. Not just watching the firefighters battle the blaze, but it's the thrill of seeing how much damage they've caused."

He hadn't considered someone would risk raising suspicion by hanging out for hours in this small town, but it was probable, considering the bomb in his truck and the aggressive nature of the fire that had been set. "The office where Aleida Martinez was found went up fast and hot with no windows for her to escape. There was no need to start two additional fires unless the goal was to ensure the whole building burned to the ground."

"If you've got a local law enforcement contact who could handle taking the photos, it would be helpful."

"As a matter of fact, I do. My brother Holden is the chief deputy in the sheriff's office." His cell phone buzzed. He pulled it from his pocket. "Speak of the devil. Give me a minute."

Liz nodded.

Sawyer answered. "I was just talking about you."

"And I was just looking at your truck," Holden said. "Or should I say what's left of it. Please tell me you're in one piece. I don't want to be the one to have to give Mom bad news."

"No worries on that front." Sawyer spun around in his chair, facing the wall and lowered his voice. "Guess who's in my office?"

"I hate suspense."

"Liz."

A long beat of silence. "Your Liz?" his brother finally asked.

It had been a long time since he'd heard anyone refer to her as his. Didn't change how he'd never stop thinking of her that way.

"I can hear you," she said in a singsong voice.

Sawyer winced. "Yep. Listen, I need a favor." He explained to Holden about the need to have a deputy take discreet photos of any crowd that gathered at future fires.

"I'll get on it as soon as we're done collecting what little forensic evidence is left out here."

"Once you get it, hang on to it. Liz has a contact at Quantico who will fast-track lab results. We're sending him everything."

"Roger that. I'm relieved you're okay. Truly. I'll see you tonight. Heads up, Grace might want to look you over."

No might about it. With Grace, Holden's wife, it was a guarantee. She was a nurse, drop-dead gorgeous and the sweetest soul, who his brother was madly in love with. There would be no hiding his injuries from her.

"I've got stitches in my side, a minor burn on my arm and a cut on my thigh," Sawyer said, coming clean.

"Smart man to fess up. It'll make her examination faster. Later."

"Thanks." They hung up and he spun back around, facing Liz.

She gave a wry grin. "You a fire marshal *and* Holden a deputy? Unreal," she said with a shake of her head.

"Actually, all of my brothers ended up in law enforcement."

Liz shot him an incredulous look. "All of you? Wow. What about Matt?"

Matt Granger was his first cousin on his mother's side. After Sawyer's aunt bankrupted her family with gambling debts and ran off with another man, Matt, who was only seven at the time, and his father came to live at the Powell ranch. Matt was raised almost like a brother rather than a cousin and his father became head manager, overseeing the cattle.

"As soon as Matt turned eighteen, he joined the army. Did black ops. Then he came back and believe it or not became a cop. He was recently promoted to chief of campus police at the local university."

"Your maternal grandfather was a cop, right?"

"A sheriff. Like his father before him. My mom planned to join the FBI after she finished her degree. Dad was going to leave Wyoming and follow her wherever she went, but my granddad got sick. My dad had to take over the Shooting Star. Then Mom got pregnant with Monty and all their plans changed."

"I didn't know. I guess law enforcement runs in your blood, but I thought for sure you boys would've taken over the family ranch. At least one of you. My money was on Monty," she said, and Sawyer would've made the same bet. "That was always your father's dream. He must be proud of you guys, but I'm sure he's also kind of disappointed."

The words tugged at his heart. His father had four sons who loved the ranch and enjoyed working on it, but they'd all been called to do something else. "Long story. The short version is my dad isn't thrilled about it but he claims to understand. I think he's secretly holding on to hope that one of us will give up the badge and take over the ranch someday."

Sawyer opened his bottom drawer and grabbed a fresh work T-shirt. As he pulled off the scrubs top, Liz's gaze slid over his body, a blush rising on her cheeks, before she looked away.

He had to check his grin, but it was nice to know he could still catch her eye. That would have to be good enough for right now.

"Walk me through the other two fires," she said.

Although Liz had a digital copy of everything on the case, he pulled out the physical file, crossed the room and sat beside her on the sofa. He set the folder on the coffee table in front of her and opened it. "The first was a restaurant. No casualties. The owner is devastated. He recently spent a boatload renovating the place. The loss financially ruined him since insurance won't cover arson. The perpetrator started a leak from a gas line, let it build and left a device to get the fire started. Caused an explosion. There wasn't much left, but when I inspected, I found remnants of a timer."

"A timer?" She looked over the file.

"Found the same at the Compassionate Hearts and the fires before that. A cabin over in Bison Ridge. I cover that town, too. Four guys hunting over the weekend. And then a nail salon. Happened after-hours when the head nail tech was doing inventory in the basement."

"Our guy loves fire but likes to set it at a safe distance. Doesn't want to risk getting burned himself. The timer also shows control. Patience. Same accelerant?"

"I believe so. Gasoline."

"What was used to ignite it?" She looked up at him.

"My guess, based on the intensity of the burn pattern at the point of origin, something really hot. I'm thinking a flare."

"Like the kind used on the road for an emergency?"

"It's possible. Easy enough to get. Certainly burns hot enough at 1,500 degrees Fahrenheit. I believe the timer was rigged to set it off. I won't know for certain about the flare or get confirmation on gasoline as the accelerant until I get the results from the lab. They're backed up as usual. Could take six to eight weeks."

She raised her eyebrows in surprise. "Long time to wait."

"Welcome to my world." He had to rely on the crime laboratory that processed forensics for the entire state. Waiting two months was standard procedure.

"Actually, let me introduce you to mine." She took out her cell and dialed a number. "Hey Ernie, this is Kelley. SAC Cho sent me to Laramie, Wyoming, to cover the—" She paused as she listened to the guy on the other end. "You saw it on the news earlier. That's the case. Yeah, lucky me," she said with a bit of a grimace. "Listen, we need assistance processing the evidence from the fires ASAP. The faster, the better on this one." Her gaze bounced up to Sawyer's. She nodded and smiled. "Thanks. I owe you one for this." She disconnected. "Once he gets it over at Quantico, he'll do his best to get us answers in less than forty-eight hours."

"Wow." He was impressed. "Must be nice having friends in high places."

"We'll need to drive over to Cheyenne and pick up what you've already submitted to DCI," she said, referring to the Division of Criminal Investigation, where the lab was located.

"No need. I can have Logan send it to your contact. He's a DCI agent. Still lives on the ranch, like me. Only he has a longer commute."

"Holden is chief deputy. Logan is with DCI. What about Monty?"

"State trooper."

"Do you all live on the ranch?" she asked with a teasing smile.

"Afraid so," he said.

Her smile spread wider. "But why? You're all rich."

Sawyer huffed a tired chuckle. "Correction, Holly and Buck Powell are rich," he said, talking about his parents. "My brothers and Matt and I are living off civil servant salaries." It wasn't as bad as it sounded. Their parents had built Monty his own house on the property after everyone thought he was going to get hitched. The engagement fell through, but the place was still there and his. Last year, Holden and his wife moved from the apartment above the garage to their own home a few acres away from Monty once construction was completed. Sawyer took the garage apartment while Logan stayed in a large room in a separate wing of the house from their parents. Matt built his own place, not wanting to stay in the main house or wait to have his aunt and uncle pay for it provided he ever got married. "Besides, Mom and Dad like having us close." It also made it easy for them to pitch in to help on the ranch when needed. "Speaking of living arrangements, where are you planning to stay while you're here?"

"Home. My mom has an old friend who looks after the place. I called her on the drive up. There'll be a key waiting for me under the front mat."

He turned toward her, and his knee brushed against hers, causing an electric spark where they touched. Holding off on a conversation about the past was one thing, but he found it impossible to ignore feelings that welled inside him every time he looked into her eyes. Feelings that reminded him of what they once had. How only physical contact with her would ease the dull ache in his heart.

Their great chemistry hadn't dissipated, but what he wanted from her wasn't sexual, or rather not only sexual. He longed for the intimacy he hadn't known since her, to hold her while she fell asleep. To listen to her breathing. To feel her heart beating against his chest.

If only she needed the same, but at least she didn't pull away this time. A good sign.

"If you get lonely out there all by yourself," he said, reaching over and putting his hand on her knee, "remember, I'm just a few acres away." On horseback, he could reach her in minutes, but that was still too far for his liking. "You could stay on the ranch if you'd prefer. Plenty of guest rooms, and I can guarantee three things—a comfy bed, hot breakfast and strong coffee. In full disclosure, I make no promises that my mom won't cater to your every whim."

A demure smile pulled at her mouth, holding back a laugh. What he wouldn't give to hear her laugh again.

"I'll be fine," she said. "I'm used to solitude."

"Just because you're used to something doesn't mean you like it. Or have to endure it. Especially not while I'm around. If you were at the ranch, it'd be easier to talk. About work. Only the case," he said, clarifying. He didn't want her to bring the wall back up between them when he'd just gotten her to lower it. "I won't push on the rest." *Only a nudge here and there.*

She hesitated, her expression tightening.

"It'd be safer for you, too," he added. "You're assuming the bomb went off early because you were there and this guy didn't want to kill a federal agent. But what if you're wrong? What if the detonator malfunctioned? What if he didn't want to kill the reporter? Egan has been giving him a lot of coverage that I'm sure he's lapping up. There are a lot of what-ifs." He'd been calculating them. Each one made her theory less likely. "If he planted a bomb in my truck because of my investigation, then you're going to be a target right along with me going forward."

"I can handle myself."

So could he, with an assailant he could see and fight. He hadn't stood a chance against a car bomb.

"You've never been targeted by someone like this," he said.

"Before I was assigned to BAU in Quantico, I worked a case undercover. I had to infiltrate an extremist group. Find their bomb maker. Some people who make explosives bear the marks of their handiwork. The bureau thought I was a perfect fit. They were right. I was able to lure him in. He was attracted to my scars. A sick, twisted guy, but when I caught him, made the bust, it hit the news. My name, my face were out there. The only good thing to come from having my identity exposed was I could publish the book I had been working on. What most people don't know, the part that didn't make it in the news, was I barely got through that alive. In the end, it came down to him and me, but I didn't let him win."

Sawyer wasn't most people. Although he lacked the resources of the FBI, he stayed abreast of what was happening in her life. He was aware of what she'd been through.

"This is different," he said. "You don't have other agents for backup, surveilling your every move."

What if this guy found out where she was staying and lit the house on fire while she was asleep? Or planted a bomb in her rental?

The horrific idea made his blood boil. Made him want to find the culprit and put an end to him before he had another chance to hurt her. He'd taken a piece of shrapnel in his side, but the door that blew off his truck had nearly taken off her head. They were both fortunate to be alive and he intended to keep it that way.

He realized the nature of her job meant sometimes she would face danger, but if it was in his power to protect her, to keep her from suffering, then he would.

"There are no houses near yours." His place was the closest, but it wasn't as if he could stick his head out the window and see her. Bison Ridge was a small mountain-town with a fairly large surrounding landscape, along with a sheriff, a general store and only a few other ranches. "Anything could happen to you out there. My family's ranch is better. Safer." No one was getting in uninvited. If by chance they did, everyone in his family was an excellent shot, thanks to his father making certain of it. Plus, they had twenty armed cowboys in the bunkhouse and a security system.

Liz stared down at his hand on her knee before putting hers atop his and giving it a small squeeze. Her mouth opened. He knew she'd protest because she was a fighter, but he had a sound rebuttal. A knock on the door stopped her from speaking.

They shifted apart.

"Come in," he said.

The door opened. Gareth McCreary poked his head in. He was the assistant chief, managing day-to-day operations, filling in for the chief or one of the battalion commanders as needed. Catching sight of Liz, he hesitated. "I don't mean to interrupt. Do you have a minute?"

Unlike Ted, Gareth was levelheaded. A relatively nice guy. Sawyer never had a problem with him, even when they were going after the same job as fire marshal. "Sure."

"Glad to see you're all right after the bomb tore your truck to pieces." Gareth stepped inside, holding an armful of turn-out gear. "We gathered your stuff for you," he said, setting it down in a chair.

"Thanks. I appreciate it." His gear had been the last thing on his mind once the ambulance had arrived and Liz had the foresight to transport the evidence. "Were you on the team today?" The assistants usually worked different shifts from the chief.

"No. When I heard about the fire, I went to check out the scene. Ted is taking off early. Engagement party planning. I'm filling in for him."

"Great." Since Gareth hovered, Sawyer asked, "Anything else I can do for you?"

"It's what I can do for you. I heard things got heated between you and Ted earlier."

Sawyer shook his head. "Not on my end."

Raising his hands in mock surrender, Gareth kept his expression neutral. "With this recent string of fires and murders, we need to remember we're on the same team. Ted agrees. As a gesture of goodwill," he said, tossing him something from his pocket.

Sawyer caught the keys to one of the station's command SUVs. "I was told there wasn't funding in the budget for me to use a department vehicle."

"You need wheels to do your job," Gareth said. "Until you wrap this case, we'll treat any fire like it might be arson. You go in before overhaul. Also—" he beckoned someone else inside "—I think you know this guy."

Joshua Burfield entered and waved hello.

"I do." Stepping over, Sawyer shook the volunteer's hand.

"I asked Josh to brief the others in the VFD," Gareth said, "to ensure we don't have any further miscommunication. The sooner you catch the sick guy doing this, the better for everyone. Including us."

"Please let the volunteers know I appreciate their efforts." Sawyer wanted to make that clear. Their assistance was essential during a crisis such as this. "I hope there are no hard feelings."

Josh shrugged. "If there are, I'm sure it'll blow over. We're here to make things easier. Not harder for anyone in the department."

"One more thing, and we'll let you two get back to it," Gareth said. "Dinner is ready in the kitchen. I volunteered to cook and picked up groceries on my way in. Spaghetti and meatballs. My mother's recipe. You two feel free to help yourself."

"Thank you," Liz said. "Very kind of you."

"Unfortunately, we've already ordered from Delgado's." Sawyer sat back on the sofa.

"If you change your mind, you know where the kitchen is," Gareth said before leaving with Josh and shutting the door behind them.

"That's a first. Make that two," Sawyer said. "I was one

of them for more than ten years, I work in the same building, and I haven't been made to feel welcome to join any meals since I started this job. Now I get a dinner invitation and keys to a department vehicle in one day."

Another knock on the door. This time it was their dinner delivery. Sawyer tipped the driver and they dug into the food.

Liz moaned. "I didn't realize how hungry I was," she said around a mouthful of food.

"Ditto." He bit into his burger.

"Or how much I missed Delgado's beef French dip sandwiches with au jus."

He hoped she'd realize there were other things and people she missed, too.

"Hey, what does Ted have against you?" Liz asked before stuffing some fries in her mouth.

How nice to see she had a healthy appetite and didn't only stick to bird food. "He thinks—well, they all think I got the job over Gareth because my last name is Powell." It was a fact and no secret that his parents had friends in high places and enough influence to give him the advantage if he and Gareth were equally qualified. It was also a fact, but a lesser-known truth, that they never would. They came from the school of hard work and had ingrained in their sons the importance of earning their achievements. The only handouts were free room and board, only to keep their kids close, but Sawyer and his brothers even paid for that by working on the ranch. He had the calluses and occasional sleep deprivation to prove it.

"If only they knew you better." Liz patted his leg. "You'd never accept a job you hadn't earned on your own merit," she said with such confidence it filled him with warmth.

She had been more than his girlfriend. More than his lover. She was his best friend. The one person outside his family who knew him, had his back and believed in him without question. Something he hadn't been able to find with anyone else. To be so completely loved. To be the center of another's life.

"Take the invitation and the vehicle as an olive branch." She set down the sandwich, wiped her hands and picked up the file.

"Lizzie, staying at your house alone—"

"If he used a timer and a flare, how did he hide it?" she asked, cutting him off.

"I believe he planted some kind of canister filled with gasoline, the timer or detonator and flare attached, all concealed in something nondescript. Like a box. At Compassionate Hearts, I found the remnants under a chair in the office and two other spots. He probably planted it the night before around the closing of the restaurant, the nail salon and the thrift store when workers were tired, eager to leave and wouldn't have noticed a small box. It would've been easier to do at the cabin in the woods."

She riffled through the pages. "Where was the device left at the salon?"

"In the basement. Near the stairwell. The fire would've blocked the only way to escape."

"Located in the back of the building?"

Sawyer nodded. "Both of them."

"Then he would've wanted to make sure the nail tech and Aleida were in the right spot when it went off. If this guy was watching, he couldn't have seen them from the street, known for certain they were where he wanted them."

Sawyer connected the dots. "Unless he'd called them. There was a phone line in the basement of the salon and office. They answer, he gets them talking, keeping them on the line until the timer goes off."

"I'll get the phone records. Maybe this guy was stupid enough not to use a burner." She flipped through a couple of pages and stiffened.

"What is it?" he asked.

The color drained from her face. "Can't be," she said, her voice barely a whisper as she stared at the page. "Look." She pointed to the four victims of the cabin fire. "Do you recognize the names? Those three?"

Sawyer glanced at the pictures and the names that went along with them, but nothing rang a bell. He was acquainted with most of the victims. More than a handful of times, he'd been in Compassionate Hearts, had spoken with Martinez in passing. He'd eaten at the restaurant before it had been renovated and burned to the ground. His mother had gotten her nails done at the salon often, and everyone there was pleasant enough. All of them, including the hunters he'd gone to high school with, though he hadn't known them. But that didn't give him the answer as to why they had been attacked.

They didn't go to the same church, belong to the same clubs or even use the same banks. Four lived in Laramie, the other two in Bison Ridge.

"What am I missing?" he asked.

"The hunters, Flynn Hartley, Scott Unger, Randy Tillman, the nail salon technician, Courtney O'Hare, and Aleida Martinez. They were all there at the summer camp the night of the fire."

Sawyer took the file from her and looked it over. He hadn't attended the camp and wasn't familiar with those who had. Though the fire had left indelible scars on the inside for him, he hadn't memorized the list of teens who had escaped. "What about the fourth hunter, Al Goldberg, and the restaurateur, Chuck Parrot? Were they there, too?"

Liz thought for a moment, squeezed her eyes shut and shook her head. "No. They weren't."

He took the file and turned to the incident where the nail tech had been killed. "What about the owner of the salon? Do you recognize the name?"

She glanced at the page. "No."

"What if the murderer had mistaken the tech for the owner and killed O'Hare by accident. This might not be what you're thinking." He hoped like hell that it wasn't.

She sucked in a deep, slow breath, and then her gaze lifted to his. "Five out of the seven people targeted were there that night. You're the math guy. Statistically, is that a coincidence? Or are we dealing with something else? Could the connection be the fire?"

"It's possible Goldberg is an outlier. A result of human error. The murderer didn't care if Goldberg was in the wrong place at the wrong time and was acceptable collateral damage in order to kill the other men. But why Parrot's restaurant?"

"Maybe our guy torched the restaurant to hide his real motive. Arsonists do it all the time. With Goldberg, perhaps it's like you said, he's an outlier. Wrong place. Wrong time."

They needed to be careful not to skew the data to fit an emotional model. The fire fifteen years ago changed the trajectory of their lives, upended their worlds. The cloud of it, hanging over their heads to this day, could be overshadowing the way she looked at the facts. "We can't jump to conclusions and see threads where there aren't any. There has to be another link we're missing between them."

Liz nodded but with a doubtful expression.

Whatever the connection, they had to find it and be certain. Fast.

Chapter Five

He checked his watch. 10:35 p.m.

Time to shake things up.

He whipped out his burner cell phone and made the call.

On the third ring, the line was answered. "Hello," Neil Steward said.

"You deserve what's about to happen."

Neil didn't respond right away. "Oh yeah, and what's that?"

"Fireworks."

"Bob, is this you messing around?"

"This isn't Bob. The fireworks and much more you deserve. Your son is a different story." The authorities would find his twenty-three-year-old son's body inside the Cowboy Way Tattoo Parlor, where he worked at his father's shop. He'd killed Mike a little earlier. Slit his throat. Then set the devices to start the fire. "But sins of the father..."

"Who is this?"

He triggered the timer and counted down in his head. "My name is Vengeance. You're guilty for what happened to Timothy. You stood by and did nothing to stop it. You stayed silent. Sold your soul. That's why I've taken your boy and your shop." To teach Neil about true loss.

"I—I—I don't know what you're talking about or what you want, but if anything happens to my son, the police are going to get involved. You hear me?"

If only he'd told the police the truth years ago, Mikey would be alive now. But then Neil wouldn't have been paid for silence or had the money to start his own tattoo shop. Neil was a liar and a coward who valued money more than doing the right thing, and when the authorities questioned him tonight, the odds were he'd even lie about this phone call.

"Listen to me, Neil. You're going to burn in hell." *Three.* "No need to call the cops." *Two.* "Your son's body will be found before long." *One.* "They'll be in touch shortly."

The fire had started. Too bad he couldn't be there to see it just yet. Soon. Patience.

Right on cue, Neil yelled colorful expletives over the line, but that wouldn't bring his son back.

He disconnected.

Neil would try to call his son first, then go looking for him at the shop.

Any minute now, a passerby on the street would smell smoke, notice the flames and dial 911. The fire department would be on the scene in less than ten minutes, and a large crowd would gather once more.

Then he could see the Cowboy Way burn.

But how long until you arrive, Liz?

LIZ PULLED UP to her family house and parked the car. *Home.* She'd always think of it as such even if she didn't want to stay.

Sawyer was right behind her in the department vehicle.

She'd declined his offer, again, to stay at the Shooting Star Ranch, but he insisted on making sure she got to her place safely.

Popping the trunk, she hopped out of the car. "See. Nothing to worry about."

"Let's check the place out, sweep for any planted devices before we issue an all clear. Okay?"

Wise words. She wouldn't protest since it had been her plan to search the house.

He reached for her bags, but she grabbed them.

"You're injured." She frowned at him. "And I'm more than capable of carrying my things. I do it all the time."

He took the bags from her hand and closed the trunk. "First, I'm fine. Second, you've been gone so long you've forgotten how a cowboy operates."

Chivalry was not dead in the Mountain West. Another thing she missed.

She led the way up the porch. Under the mat, she found the key and unlocked the door.

Sawyer's phone rang. As they stepped inside, he answered, "Hello." He got quiet as he listened, his features tightening with worry. "You've got to be kidding me." More silence. "We'll be there as soon as we can." He hung up. "There's another fire."

"Already? We extrapolated that there wouldn't be another for a day or two. Not in less than twenty-fours. It's too soon."

"I don't care about FBI projections. I care about the firefighters. The team is exhausted from putting out and over-hauling the one at Compassionate Hearts. Not only are innocent civilians being killed, but with this grueling pace of these attacks, the lives of firefighters are being jeopardized."

After they stepped outside, she locked the front door. "Where is it?"

"Back in Laramie. Town center."

Thirty minutes away.

"I'll drive," he said, heading for the SUV.

BITING BACK A SMILE, he watched Liz Kelley climb out of the red LFD SUV and fall into step beside Sawyer, her gaze glued to the fiery beast devouring the Cowboy Way Tattoo Parlor.

Magnificent.

As much as he wanted to stare at the flames and savor the devastation on Neil Steward's face, he kept Liz in sight.

FBI was printed in bright yellow letters on the jacket she wore like armor. The same way she wore the scarf that hid her puckered skin. Relying on her attractive face to appear normal when she was anything but. Covering up her scars when she should've exposed them with pride. The marks of a survivor.

All proof she was still clinging to who she had once been—a pretty, vapid doll, good for nothing besides spreading her legs for Sawyer—instead of embracing what the fire made her, forged into someone new.

A wasted gift. One he'd take back.

It was no coincidence Liz was in town.

Providence brought her to Laramie. Vulcan, the god of fire, summoned her...just for him.

At first, when he spotted her in front of the smoking heap of what was left of Compassionate Hearts, it had been a shock. Then his surprise slowly twisted to anticipation.

Years ago, he thought Liz would be the one to get away. The fire had taken everything from her. Left her scarred and scared. On the run from life itself, which had been sweeter than killing her. But here she was, bigwig FBI agent, risen like a phoenix from the ashes, returned right on time.

Back on his list with the others who would pay.

Earlier, he had salivated at the idea of taking her out along with Sawyer Powell in one fell swoop with the truck bomb, the remote detonator itching in his hand.

But the reporter, covering his handiwork with such flourish, had been with them. Gave him reason to reconsider. So he'd set it off early and got to witness how the air shook with the explosion, glass bursting from the windows, flames lapping at the metal. The second concussive blast was better than the first, with the truck door nearly decapitating Liz and shrapnel wounding Sawyer.

Good thing they hadn't died quickly and painlessly.

The explosion gave him insight. In the aftermath, watching them—how Sawyer tried to shield Liz, the way she caressed his face, the worry in her eyes before she ran to her car, no doubt to race to the hospital—was like old times. Something still burned between them.

Sawyer was a nuisance that he simply wanted out of the way, but with Liz, he could do something special. Toy with her. Break her. Take away someone she loved to show her how it felt before he killed her.

Even if she was FBI.

He wasn't a fool and didn't need the Feds breathing down his neck. So he'd wait until she left Wyoming to end her. After all, he was a patient man. Better to torch her in Virginia anyway. Then her death wouldn't appear related.

Finishing the list and keeping his promise would be worth it in the end. It was the only way to get what he wanted. Needed more than anything else in the world.

Staring at Liz, he knew exactly how to have fun with her while he bided his time to kill her.

He wondered if she could feel the heat of his flame standing so close or sensed what was to come.

Chapter Six

"Is it our guy?" Liz approached Sawyer, who had snagged Gareth's attention as the assistant chief came out of the tattoo shop. "Did he do it again?"

Gareth moved them farther away from the building. "It appears so."

"What happened?" Sawyer asked.

"The owner of the shop next door smelled smoke, went outside to check it out and reported the fire at about 10:40 p.m. Our company and the VFD responded at 10:47 p.m. and 10:55 p.m., respectively. Once we got inside, I immediately saw the similarity to the other fires. That's when I came back out and called you. After I hung up, I heard Neil Steward, the owner, screaming that his kid, Mike, was inside." Gareth gestured to the poor man. "His wife, Evelyn."

Horror and sad resignation welled in Steward's glassy eyes as he held his wife, who was sobbing.

Liz swore under her breath. Her heart ached with pity for the couple.

"Two went in to look for him," Gareth said. "The pair checked the first floor where they do the tattoos, but he wasn't there."

"Did they search the basement or office?" Sawyer asked.

"The office is on the second floor. Can't get close enough

yet. Two more devices went off near a pile of flammable materials that were in the shop."

Dread slithered up Liz's spine. "Has that happened before, devices going off while you were inside?"

Gareth shook his head. "No. First time."

"Were the devices exposed or were they hidden inside anything?" Sawyer asked.

"Concealed in cardboard boxes."

Sawyer sighed. "This guy is escalating things. Deliberately endangering firefighters."

"Well," Gareth said, tipping his hat back, "he's definitely slowing us down."

"Strange," Sawyer muttered, staring at the blaze.

She studied his face. "What is it?"

"Our guy wanted the other places to burn to the ground. Hot and fast. Why not this one?" Sawyer mused. "With the other devices going off later, he wanted to take his time for some reason."

Turning, Liz stared at the tormented looks on the faces of Mr. and Mrs. Steward, their gazes fixed on the inferno that had once been their business. "Maybe it's not about the firefighters. I can't imagine anything worse for a parent than this. Having to watch the fire that has taken away their livelihood while waiting to find out if their child is alive or dead."

She scanned the crowd. This guy was out there, taking it all in, relishing the pain and devastation he caused. No way he'd miss it.

Liz spotted someone on the periphery of the crowd discreetly taking pictures. A woman with an athletic build and long hair in a ponytail. "Hey, is that a deputy in plain clothes?" she asked Sawyer.

He followed her gaze. "Deputy Ashley Russo."

"Good." Liz nodded once, briskly. "We'll have a picture of him. He's here. I'm sure of it."

Sawyer leaned in, putting his mouth close to her ear. "The Stewards, were any of them in the fire at the camp—Neil, Evelyn or Mike?"

"They weren't there." She knew the names of every camper that had been locked in the cabins and all the men from the bunkhouse who had worked to save her life and rescue the Durbins that night.

How were the Stewards connected to the other recent victims?

Two firefighters emerged from the tattoo parlor.

"We want to talk to them," Sawyer said to Gareth.

"Come on. It's Anderson and the probie Johnson. Hey!" Gareth started toward the fire engine where the two were headed. "Anderson, Johnson, over here!"

The two turned and trudged toward them in full turnout gear with their breathing apparatuses hanging around their necks. One was a woman, which surprised Liz. She wasn't sure why. In her job, she'd met more than a few female firefighters. Maybe she hadn't expected to find one here in Laramie.

Both had looks of weary devastation.

"Anderson, Johnson," Sawyer said, "this is Agent Liz Kelley. Well? Did you find Mike Steward?"

"We thought we had a chance of saving him," Anderson said, her voice rough from the smoke. "The fire didn't reach the second floor. We managed to put it out, but he was already dead."

"Smoke inhalation?" Sawyer asked.

Johnson shook his head. "His throat had been cut. I thought I was going to retch right there. Never seen anything like it."

"Me either. My God." Anderson's voice was heavy, horrified. "Do you think the fire was set to cover it up?" she asked.

"He wanted us to find the body like that." Liz crossed her arms. "Otherwise, he would've set a device upstairs. Probably would have doused it in gasoline, too, to hide the wound until the ME examined the body."

"Tell me what you saw when you first went in," Sawyer said.

"Not much at first." Anderson opened the top part of her coat. "Smoke was too thick. Black."

"The spray turned to vapor straight away," Johnson added.

"You should know the fire was up high, Sawyer," Anderson said. "In certain areas, the ceiling looked the same as the recent fires."

"He used gasoline again."

"Same accelerant," Anderson said with a nod. "The others got a handle on the secondary fires." She tugged off her gloves. "We kept moving. Checked the basement first since we found the nail tech down there. But nothing. We finally got up to the second floor."

Johnson closed his eyes. "I almost—" he paused and swallowed convulsively "—slipped in the blood. There was so much."

"It's not an easy sight," Liz said, trying to console him. "Even if you've seen it before, you never really get used to it."

Anderson looked at Sawyer. "Got a second?" She hiked her chin to the side, and they took a couple of steps away.

"You all right, Tessa?" He pushed her hat back and put a comforting hand on her shoulder, and unwelcome annoyance prickled Liz.

"I've been better." Even dirty with a soot-smudged face, she was girl-next-door cute. "When my shift from hell ends,

I really need to blow off some steam. Decompress. You interested in having some fun tomorrow night?"

One side of Sawyer's mouth hiked up in a wry grin.

The idea of him having fun with the pretty, probably flawless, firefighter sent a wave of jealousy through Liz so hard and fast it astonished her.

Get a grip. Although she had been living like a nun, there was zero reason for a handsome hottie like Sawyer Powell to be celibate. Girls had been throwing themselves at him since high school. He'd had his pick, could've chosen anyone, but he'd fallen for her. She'd been truly lucky then, before the fire.

Sawyer probably had a lot of *fun* on a regular basis, and it was none of her business. Only this case was.

Giving herself a stern mental shake, she looked away as Sawyer replied to Tessa too low for Liz to hear and turned to Gareth. "Has anybody talked to the crowd?"

"Yeah, Sawyer's brother Holden." Gareth looked around. "He's out there somewhere."

"I'll find him."

"Hey." Gareth stopped her from walking away. "We didn't really know each other well back in the day."

She tensed, bracing herself for it. She'd run into more people from high school than she cared to remember since she'd been back. Gareth was going to be the first to bring up the fire. "We didn't hang out in the same circles. But I hear you and Ted are still best friends."

Whenever you saw one, you saw the other. Frick and Frack was what everyone called them in school.

Odd how things and people she hadn't thought of in ages were coming back to her now.

Gareth's smile was tight and didn't reach his eyes. "Ted

can come across a bit abrasive." He lifted a brow. "But he's a good guy."

"If you say so."

He met her gaze squarely. "Anyway, what happened to you back then was awful. It's good to see you again, doing so well."

"Yeah." She never knew how to respond when all she wanted was to walk away. "Thanks."

"Hotshot FBI. I bought a copy of your book. Most of us at the station did. It's signed, but before you leave town, would you mind personalizing it for me?"

Inwardly, she cringed but kept her discomfort from surfacing on her face.

Sawyer left Tessa Anderson's side.

"Sure, I'll sign it if you want. Excuse me." Liz stepped away from Gareth. "Sounds like you've got a hot date tomorrow night." As soon as the words left her mouth, she regretted saying them. *Why did you go there?*

He stopped and stared at her. "Do you care?" he shot back, his gaze boring into hers.

She shouldn't, but she did. "You're free to do what you want when you're not working. Everyone needs downtime to blow off steam. You deserve it."

"That includes you, too, right?"

Nice going. "I'll go for a run. It's how I unwind. I'll be fine."

"You're fine a lot. Fine working for the FBI. Fine out in Virginia. Fine with your solitude. Fine staying at that old house in Bison Ridge alone regardless of the risks. Fine going for a run instead of getting sweaty with someone. But are you ever happy, Lizzie?"

She rocked back on her heels. Why was she suddenly under attack? And how dare he analyze her and try to dissect her life. "I shouldn't have made the comment about the hot date. It's not my business. I wasn't judging."

Sighing, he lowered his head. "I'm glad you said something. It's the only way I'd know if you cared." His gaze flickered back up to hers. "And, no, I don't have a date. Tessa claims she wants fun, but I know better. What she really wants is a husband."

"You'd make a great one. You're the settling-down type. Clearly you two have chemistry."

A muscle ticked in his jaw. "Chemistry isn't the same as compatibility. No marriage should be based on sex. Even if it is mind-blowing."

Not only did he have fun with Tessa, but it was *mind-blowing*. A detail she did not need or want to know.

"Bottom line," he continued, "I'm not the guy for her and she's not the woman for me. Not that you care though, right?"

Movement from the corner of her eye told her this conversation wasn't private.

She pivoted and faced Holden Powell.

"Sorry to intrude. I didn't realize," Holden said to Sawyer. "Hey, you." He wrapped her in a big hug, lifting her from her feet.

It was unexpected and warm and lasted way too long.

Finally, he put her down, leaving her breathless. She wasn't used to affection anymore, much less the big, cowboy kind.

"It's been ages since I've seen you," Holden said.

She pulled up her scarf that had slipped down her neck. "Yeah." She glanced at Sawyer, but he didn't meet her eyes, wouldn't even look at her. Did she want him to?

Staring at him, she no longer knew *what* she wanted besides solving this case.

"I need to go inside the shop." Sawyer turned for the department SUV, with Liz and Holden following behind him. He grabbed his boots from the trunk and sat on the tailgate.

Liz watched him slip them on, his jaw clenched, his fingers clumsy on the clamps of the boots. This type of emotional distraction, worrying about him and herself, rather than concentrating on the job, was precisely what she wanted to avoid. It was bad enough that doubt always found a way to slide in regardless of how many cases she closed. For her, there were always waves of self-confidence with an undercurrent of insecurity. She didn't need complicated emotions thrown into the mix. "This is why I wanted to keep things professional. Not make it personal. Can you let this go?"

Giving a chuckle full of ire, he grabbed his kit. "*You* brought up *me* having a hot date," he snapped. "You got personal. But sure, I can let it go. I'll store it in my locked box where I keep everything else bottled up until I have your permission to unpack it."

Holden whistled softly.

She opened her mouth to set him straight, and her mind went blank. Except for one thing. He was right. About all of it. Her focus had slipped. She'd gotten jealous when she had no right and then opened a giant can of worms by discussing it.

Liz let out a long breath.

Holden put a hand on his brother's shoulder. "Are you okay to go in there injured? You've got stitches."

"I'm medically cleared to do my job, Mom." Shoving past them, Sawyer flipped on a flashlight and stalked off into what remained of the tattoo shop, carrying his kit.

"Man, you got him riled up." Holden elbowed her. "Deep down, he's just happy to have you back in town."

"I can tell." She looked up at him. He was a little shorter than Sawyer and no longer broader. When Holden played football, he was beefy. Since then, he'd gotten leaner, which suited him. He was clean-shaven. None of the scruffy rough-and-tumble two-day stubble Sawyer had down so well, making him look edgy.

Holden stared at her with those kind eyes of his and flashed a sympathetic smile. "You've been gone too long."

"Or not long enough."

"He always swore you'd come back. And here you are. Getting a wish fulfilled after fifteen years is a lot to process when you're simultaneously investigating the toughest case of your career alongside the woman who was the love of your life."

But she didn't come back for him. A pang of guilt lanced her chest.

Get to work. She bit down on the inside of her lip and refocused on the task at hand. "What did you learn from the crowd?"

"Not too much. The hours at the shop varied. According to the owner of the store next door, Mike didn't take many walk-ins. Mostly appointments. Whoever did this might have made one to get him here when he wanted. No one saw or heard anything suspicious other than the smoke. You'll want to speak to Neil Steward. He claims he received a strange phone call. Someone threatened to hurt Mike. Hard to get more out of him right now. Might be best to speak to him tomorrow."

Gareth was giving the Stewards the news about their son. The wife wailed and Neil broke down in tears. The couple needed a chance to grieve.

"Yeah. Can you ask them to come in?" she asked.

"Sure. Is the sheriff's office okay?"

She nodded. "Could you also go through the pictures Deputy Russo is taking? See if anyone stands out for any reason?"

"We'll take care of it."

"Chief Deputy! Miss FBI!" A man pushed through the crowd and slipped under the police barricade. He was holding an open bottle of whiskey. "It's high time you put a stop to this!" He took a long swig from the bottle.

Liz couldn't put a name on the face, but she recognized him.

"Chuck." Holden approached him. "I can't have you drunk and disorderly on the streets with an open container."

"I've lost everything. The restaurant. My house that I put up for collateral on the loans. Penny is gone, too. Packed a bag. Went to her mother's in Nebraska. And you want to give me a citation for trying to drown my troubles when you all should be putting a stop to this."

"Mr. Parrot, I'm Agent Liz Kelley."

"Everybody knows who you are. The girl who survived." He put the bottle up to his mouth and guzzled more liquor until Holden snatched it from his hands. Chuck lifted his chin, his eyes narrowed. Cold. Furious. Drunk. "When are you going to arrest Kade Carver?"

Holden put a fist on his hip. "What does he have to do with this?"

"Everything." Parrot threw his arms out wide and teetered. "He's the reason this is happening."

"Who is Kade Carver?" she asked, whispering to Holden.

"A wealthy developer."

"More like business wrecker," Parrot said, his words slurred. "He wants to buy out the entire block. Build a fancy townhouse community. Right here. In the center of it all. My restaurant. The nail salon. Now Neil's tattoo parlor. On the same damn block. Come on. Wake up and smell the conspiracy. With these fires, he'll get everything on this block dirt cheap now. I'm talking pennies on the dollar."

Liz looked at Holden. "Another name to add to the list for tomorrow." She glanced at Parrot. "We'll look into it."

"About time that you do." Parrot spun around, stumbled, swayed and lumbered away.

"Be prepared," Holden said. "Carver will lawyer up. It's going to be an exhausting day. Double shift for me since I'm in charge of the office while my brother-in-law is on vacation with his fiancée."

Liz patted his shoulder. "Congratulations on getting hitched. I'm glad you finally found someone willing to put up with you," she said, and he laughed. Then she pieced together what he'd said. "Wait a minute, your brother-in-law is the sheriff?"

He nodded. "My relationship with Grace happened fast and unexpectedly. It made things awkward at work for a while, but her brother has come around since the wedding. Now he's at the ranch all the time for family dinners. Anyway, where are you staying? B&B in town? The Shooting Star?"

"Bison Ridge."

Holden frowned at her. "After the car bomb, is it wise to stay out there alone?"

Ugh. "Not you, too. If I were a man, would you ask me that?"

He shrugged. "Maybe. I've always thought of you as a sister, and considering what nearly happened to Sawyer, I don't want any member of my family who is investigating this case staying somewhere isolated."

"I appreciate the concern, but I'll be fine." After all, she was a trained agent and armed.

Smiling, Holden shook his head. "You're just as stubborn as ever. Nice to see some things never change. You should get some rest."

If only. She'd been up since three that morning with nerves over her presentation at the symposium. "I've got to wait on Sawyer since we came together." *Joined at the hip.*

Holden raised his eyebrows. "Going to be a long ride to Bison Ridge with Mr. Grumpy Pants."

"Yeah. It is." But there were more important things to think about. "Come on. I'll help you finish canvassing the crowd."

Chapter Seven

A shotgun racking nearby made Sawyer jackknife upright from his sleeping bag. The sharp signature ratcheting sound, which couldn't be mistaken for anything else, had him wide awake. In the morning light filtering into his tent, he grabbed the pistol at his side.

"Whoever is in there," Liz said from outside, "come out slowly with your hands up, or I'll shoot first and ask questions later, provided you're still alive to answer."

Hearing her voice calmed his racing pulse. Exchanging his gun for his Stetson, he put his black cowboy hat on and climbed out of the tent, wearing nothing else but his boxer briefs and a smile. "Good morning to you, too."

Eyes flaring wide, Liz lowered the shotgun. Irritation etched across her face. She wore jeans, a tank top and an open button-down shirt that she had probably thrown on in haste. Her gaze dipped, traveling over his body, and a blush rose on her cheeks.

"When you dropped me off last night," she said, meeting his eyes, "and didn't hassle me again about staying out here alone, I thought you had dropped the issue."

His temper had simmered on the ride back, and he'd thought it best to be quiet. No point arguing. Nothing would've been achieved. She'd made up her mind to be stubborn, and he had made up his to be equally obstinate. "Guess you don't know me so well anymore. I told you, now that you're a part of the investigation, you could become a target as well. It's not safe for you to be out here by yourself."

"So you decided to pitch a tent in the thicket a couple hundred feet from my house and spy on me. I'm FBI. You didn't think I'd notice?"

He chuckled. "You say 'spy,' I say 'protect.' And you didn't notice my camouflaged tent until the sun came up and you were staring out the window while making coffee."

She narrowed her eyes. "How do you know that?"

Educated supposition. She was dressed and he could see the steam rising from a mug she'd left on the porch railing. "Guess I still know you pretty well."

Yawning, he stretched, and her gaze raked over him once more, making him smile.

She put a fist on her lean hip. "I'm tempted to knock that grin off your face."

"Feel free to indulge." Tipping his hat at her, he stepped within striking distance. All she had to do was reach out and touch him. "When it comes to physical contact, I'll take what I can get with you."

She leveled a look at him, hard ice in her eyes, her expression beyond chilling, but he still felt the heat from being near her. "You're incorrigible," she said, "and you're trespassing."

"Correction. You're trespassing. Ten feet before you reach the thicket is where your property line ends and mine begins." He pointed it out. "You're standing on Powell land."

Shaking her head, she sighed. "I forgot how much of it my parents sold. On the bright side, the parcel is probably small enough to put up a high fence to keep prowlers from spying."

No fence would keep him out where Liz was concerned. "I'd strongly encourage it. The investment would mean you intend to stick around." He would love nothing more than to have her stay.

Her gaze fell, the humor draining from her face. She spun around, heading back to the house, carrying the shotgun on her shoulder.

"Can I get a cup of coffee? And take a shower?" he called out after her.

Stopping, she looked back at him. "Are you kidding me?"

He shrugged. "It'll save me from driving all the way back to the ranch." His vehicle was parked down the road, but a ten-minute ride one way. "More efficient to get ready here."

She had always been a stickler about efficiency. He hoped he'd pushed the right button.

Liz considered it a moment before waving to him to follow her.

Bingo. Smiling, he ducked back into his tent. He put on his boots, grabbed his weapon and a small duffel bag with essentials and then hurried to catch up.

In the kitchen, she set the gun on a large wooden farmhouse-style table. The place brought back memories. Most of them fond. Laughter around the table at dinner with her parents. Some of them steamy. Sneaking upstairs and making out in her room. The last few memories had been heart-wrenching.

"Did your parents leave it here?" He gestured to the shotgun.

"No, the caretaker left it for me, along with a stocked fridge." She took a mug from the cabinet and filled it with steaming black coffee. "You still take two sugars and cream?"

"I wish." He patted his stomach. "Not anymore." He was trying to keep the love handles away. "I usually just add a little protein powder to it these days, but black is fine."

She picked up a resealable bag filled with a cream-colored powder from the side of the sink. "I carry some with me whenever I travel. Better than relying on burgers every time I need a quick meal." She set it on the table. "Whatever you're doing, it's clearly working," she said, eyeing his torso and handing him the mug.

As he took it from her, their fingers brushed, and he let the contact linger. "Why did your parents keep this place?" he asked, already knowing the answer. "They never come here."

She dropped her hand. "It's been in the family forever. They want me to move back here someday. Pass the place down to my children. I keep telling them I'm never getting married or having kids, but hope springs eternal with them."

His gaze fell to her exposed throat. The side was a shade lighter than the rest with discernible scars that disappeared beneath her shirt. He took in the rest of her, silky hair reflecting the sunlight, tempting cleavage, trim waist, long legs that had once curled around his hips, holding him close.

She reached for the scarf on the table.

Setting down his coffee with one hand, he caught her wrist in his other before she could take the neckerchief. "You don't need to hide from me."

She tensed. "Habit. I hate when people stare."

"I wasn't staring," he said, honestly. "I was admiring all of you." Also the truth.

A soft laugh of disbelief came from her as she rolled her eyes. "You don't have to say things like that."

She tried to pull away, but he tightened his grip. Nothing forceful. She could release the hold if she wanted. No doubt she could knock him on his butt, too, in the process.

"Why won't you ever get married or have kids?" He stepped toward her, erasing the space between them. "You're also the settling-down type." He kept his tone gentle. "You'd make a great wife. An amazing mother. You always wanted your own family."

She reeled back with a grimace, but not hard enough or far enough to break the contact. "Stop it. You know why I can't."

He drew closer, putting her arm against his chest and flattening her palm over his heart. "I don't."

"We agreed not to talk about this." Her voice was firm, but she trembled. "About us."

"I'm not talking about us. I'm asking about you," he said, his voice low and soft. "When was the last time you let someone hug you, hold you?"

His confidential source had told him Liz didn't date. Ever. Didn't hang out with friends after work. No bestie to turn to for comfort. Only traveled for business. Didn't visit her parents. A workaholic who chose to be alone.

She hesitated, and he saw in the startled depths of her pale green eyes that it had been far too long. Years.

His heart ached for her. He at least eased his pain, the loneliness, by seeking temporary comfort with others. A warm body here and there. A distraction, a reminder of what he truly missed. It always brought him full circle in the end. Right back to wanting the one person who no longer wanted him. Liz.

"A few hours ago," she stammered.

He chuckled when he really wanted to grit his teeth at how his brother had gotten his arms around her first. Born eleven months apart, with Holden being older, they'd competed most of their lives. His brother usually came out on top. But the win of hugging *his* Liz first irked him to the bone. "Holden doesn't count."

"I say he does." Her eyes hardened. "Don't you need to get ready so we can get going? We have work to do."

This case was important. No doubt about that. Lives were at risk. Another fire could be set, another murder committed at any moment. But now he realized that she didn't simply bury herself in work, she used it as a deflection, as the greatest excuse. She'd survived the fire, but she wasn't truly living.

Deep down, if he was honest, neither was he. Like recognized like.

"I think we both need something else first." He wrapped his arms around her, bringing her into his body for a hug.

She stilled, and he thought she might pull away, but she didn't. At first, she was so stiff he could have been hugging a statue. Slowly, her body relaxed against him. He tucked her head under his chin, where she fit perfectly. Resting her cheek on his shoulder, she kept one palm on his chest, spread her fingers wide and brought her other hand to his lower back, not quite returning the hug, but he'd take it.

The searing heat from having skin on skin, hers on his, sent sensation coursing through him, warming his heart, releasing the tension he carried in his chest. He wanted to tear down the protective wall she'd built around herself. The one that kept her isolated. Surround her with light and love and affection. All the things she denied herself and deserved.

Tightening the embrace, not wanting to ever let her go, he pressed his mouth to the top of her head. Inhaled the scent of her hair, breathing her in. She smelled like spring flowers after a storm. Heady. Sultry.

Sweet.

Her spine of steel softened, her body melting into his, triggering every cell in his brain to remember the passion and pleasure they'd known in each other's arms. As well as the peace. With his thumb, he made soothing circles on her back over her shirt, dipping lower. His other hand drifted to her waist and then slid to her hip. Tenderness turned to desire in a flash. No holding back. No hiding his arousal. He soaked in the heat from her body, the softness of her curves, the smell of her.

"Liz." Only a rasp of her name filled with the longing that was growing inside him.

She sighed against his chest.

The sound slight, hinting at the vulnerability she dared show, only stoked the wild need firing in his blood. She was everything he remembered. Everything he never stopped wanting. No matter how hard he had tried to get her out of his head, each time he'd failed.

She lifted her chin, their gazes locking, and she shuddered against him.

"You smell good," he whispered. *Feel good, too. Oh, so good.*

They were different people. Things had changed between them. They'd attempted to move on. But there was no denying they had grown in the same direction. Fighting for justice. Sacrificing everything to see it served. Through it all, this remained—heat and longing—the memories that wouldn't let either of them go. The feel of her against him, beneath him, when he was inside her. The taste of her in his mouth. The scent of her. The thousand little things about *her* he simply couldn't forget.

"You smell like you need a shower," she replied.

Chuckling, he cupped the side of her face, his palm cradling her cheek. "It was hot in the tent." Sweltering. Between making sure Liz was safe and the warm night air, he'd barely rested.

"You've gotten soft if you missed the AC."

They had slept under the stars more than once, enjoying not only the summer heat but also what they generated together. Sweat coating their skin, dripping from their bodies as they cuddled close. He'd taken it for granted that he'd have endless moments of holding her.

If only he'd known…

He ran his thumb over her mouth. Her lips parted with a tremble, her green eyes burning with unsure desire. Gravity pulled his head to hers, and he did what he'd longed to since he'd seen her at Compassionate Hearts. He kissed her, soft and subtle. She froze, making his heart pound with fear. Then her arms were around his neck as she rose on the balls of her feet and kissed him back, her tongue seeking his. Everything quickly became insistent, far more demanding. She arched against him, moaning, and he forgot how she'd walked away, turned her back on him, abandoned their plans for the future, forsaking him to uncertainty and a new kind of devastation. The heartache that had only deepened over time. Left him hollow. Uneasy. Aching.

Until this moment.

Her hands tangled in his hair, her body rubbing against his. He gloried in the surrender of her response. Oh, he'd miss this…missed her so much. Need rocked through him. He slid his hand from her jaw, cupping the side of her neck, wanting her even closer.

She stiffened and shoved him away. "I can't."

His heart squeezed at those two words. "Liz." Desperation was a cold hard fist in the pit of his stomach. "Please. I'm—"

"I can't," she repeated in a harsh whisper, tears glistening in her eyes, but her hands were curled into fists at her sides.

She was ready to charge into battle—against him.

But he didn't have a clue how to fight whatever this was. For so long, he thought she needed time. Needed to heal. Needed to regain her confidence. Needed to remember how strong she was. All of which she'd done.

"Can't what?" he demanded. Bear to be touched? Bear to be seen? Bear to love him anymore?

Pressure swelled in his chest like a balloon inflating.

"Do *this*." Pulling her shoulders back, she wiped any emotion from her face, her expression turning guarded. "There's no room for distraction."

His stomach dropped. That's what she thought of him, of fate bringing them back together? "This here, you and me, was once everything. Never a distraction."

"That was then. We can't repeat the past. Not everything we want deep inside works out."

Her words landed on his heart like hailstones.

Proof of what she'd said stood right in front of him. Rejecting him. Using work as an excuse.

She grabbed her holstered sidearm, sheathed knife, field jacket and scarf. "I'll meet you at the sheriff's office. I don't want to be late for any interviews." She stormed outside, letting the screen door slam shut.

Once more leaving him alone, sucking all the air out of the room. He couldn't breathe.

For years, he'd pushed forward, battling his own demons by becoming a firefighter and then fire marshal. As if putting out enough fires, saving enough people, stopping enough arsonists, would make up for his failure at keeping her safe. Change the fact that he hadn't gone into the stables after her, and if he had, the beam wouldn't have fallen on her and she wouldn't have been burned. That the universe would bring her back to him.

All the while, he refused to get attached to anyone else because no other woman was Liz. *His* Liz.

He'd waited for this chance to show her how much he still cared. That the accident didn't matter. And he blew it.

Thinking it would be simple. Easy. As if a hug and a kiss would change anything. He didn't know what in the world had come over him besides pure instinct. Standing in that kitchen like they'd done many times before, unable to keep his distance from her, he hadn't thought. The need to touch her had been all-consuming.

Nothing else had mattered. Not even the consequences.

Regret pooled in his gut, making him sick. He'd pushed too hard, too far, too fast and she ran away from him. Again.

Only this time, she was more out of reach than ever, and he had no idea what to do other than get back to work.

Chapter Eight

In the car, Liz couldn't stop shaking as she drove. She'd made a deal with him, had drawn a line in the sand, and he'd crossed it. No, he'd completely erased it. Even worse, she'd let him. Sure, he weaponized his good looks, standing in her kitchen only wearing his underwear, cowboy hat and boots. Oozing charm. Flexing his muscles. The sight of him, showing all that skin, was more temptation than any woman could resist. Even a hardened agent like her.

Crossing the line with him had been impulsive and wrong, despite feeling so right. He'd stopped her from grabbing her scarf and looked at her with those baby blues, turning her stomach fluttery, the same way he used to, the tingle spreading to her thighs. One touch, one look, and he slipped past the defenses she'd painstakingly built. She was at a loss as he wrapped her in his strong arms, the warmth of him seeping beneath her skin, the smell of him—pine and sweat, all man—enveloping her senses, completely overwhelming her, the sensations stripping her bare.

In that moment, it was impossible to make herself numb. To pretend she was fine being alone. To ignore the throbbing ache in her soul, a wound of her own making when she ended things with him.

Then he kissed her, melting her like warm butter, awakening something deep inside her that had been dormant for so long. His mouth familiar, like coming home, and at the same time new—an adventure she yearned for without realizing.

She couldn't breathe, couldn't think. Everything faded besides him and the burning need to be held by him, caressed and cherished, and to forget about the scars.

No matter how far she ran, how busy she stayed, the one truth she couldn't escape in his arms was how much she still loved him. How she wanted him more than her next breath.

But when his hand slid to her neck, she remembered why she'd left Wyoming. Why she'd left him.

Sawyer was deadly handsome. He deserved a partner who was equal in every way.

He had no idea what she looked like without clothes. Touching her, he remembered the girl she'd once been. Never quite as picture-perfect as him but overall attractive. Appealing.

Now, her body looked like a patchwork quilt from the grafts. Some areas smooth, some goosefleshy, others mottled. Almost Frankensteinesque. The sight of her nude nothing less than tragic.

She could track terrorists, infiltrate an extremist group undercover, subdue a suspect twice her size. What she could not do was risk baring herself to him, seeing pity or revulsion in his eyes, feeling hesitation in his touch.

That would break her into a million pieces with no way for her to recover.

She parked at the Sheriff's Department and took time collecting herself. *Only the case matters. Treat him like a colleague. Not a former lover who you miss more than anything in the world.* She needed another minute. Or two. Closing her eyes, she fell back on her training and shut down her emotions.

After tying the scarf around her neck and buttoning up

her shirt, she headed inside. She approached a deputy sitting at the front counter and flashed her badge. "Agent Kelley here to see Chief Deputy Powell."

"He's not in yet, but Deputy Russo is waiting for you in the sheriff's office. We were given instructions to let you and the fire marshal set up in there. Come on through."

With a nod, she said, "Thanks."

The deputy hit a buzzer, and she entered through a half door at the end of the counter. She made her way through the bullpen to the sheriff's office and knocked on the door.

Deputy Russo, in uniform, hopped up from behind the desk and greeted her at the threshold. "Pleasure to meet you. I'm Ashley Russo." She extended her hand.

The shake was firm. "Agent Kelley."

"We left a message for Mr. Carver late last night. He called bright and early this morning to say he would swing by on his way to a worksite with his attorney. Sometime this afternoon."

He was lawyering up, but at least he wasn't stalling. Her gut told her he'd have a solid alibi. His type always did. "What about Mr. and Mrs. Steward?"

"They said they'd come in but didn't commit to a specific time."

Completely understandable. The horror of what they'd been through was unimaginable, something no parent should have to suffer. "You were the one taking photographs of the crowd last night. Have you had a chance to look through them?" Liz asked.

"Yes, I have. I came in at seven to get started on it. I pulled them up on the computer. Also, I enlarged them, focusing on individual faces and printed those for you. I started putting names to a couple. There's still a lot to go through."

Overachiever. Liz liked that. "By any chance, would you be able to continue helping this morning?"

"As a matter of fact, I can. Those were my marching orders from Deputy Powell." She glanced at the clock. "He should be in soon." Russo went around the desk and pulled the chair out for her.

Liz sat and clicked through all the photos, getting oriented. Russo showed her the ones of individuals that had been enlarged and enhanced. Some had a strip of general-purpose masking tape on them with names written in Sharpie. She took in the various expressions, searching for any that stood out. Unemotional. Excited. Aroused. Happy.

"What are we working on?" a familiar voice asked from the doorway, stirring more than the physical in her.

She looked up to see Sawyer Powell waltz into the office sporting his cowboy hat, fire marshal T-shirt and jeans that highlighted his sculpted physique. Her blood pressure spiked at how good he looked. His holstered sidearm and badge hooked to his belt reminded her that not only was he a fire marshal but also a law enforcement officer.

His gaze met hers, and instead of fight in his eyes, she only saw sadness, a haunted and desolate expression hanging on his face that stunned her.

"Putting names to the faces in the crowd last night in front of the Cowboy Way," she said.

"Find anything interesting yet?" Holden asked, coming in behind his brother.

Liz glanced back at the photos. "Not yet. Russo and I could use help identifying people. I'd say the more, the merrier, but really, it'd only be faster."

"I can help for a bit." A cell phone buzzed. "I got a text from Logan," Holden said, glancing at his phone. "He is about to board a plane to drop off the evidence at Quantico.

His boss insisted on preserving the chain of custody. Nobody wants any issues if we're able to take this to trial."

"Great." The news was the best she could've hoped for, but she couldn't muster more than a humdrum response while looking at Sawyer. "Ernie will get started on it today."

As Sawyer approached the desk, she noticed he was carrying a take-out tray with two cups and a bag from Delgado's. He set one of the to-go cups down in front of her. "This is better than the sludge they perk here."

"Hey." Holden elbowed Sawyer's good side. "It's not that bad."

"Yes, it is." Sawyer opened the bag and set two wrapped sandwiches on the desk. "Breakfast. Egg whites and cheese. One has turkey bacon. The other turkey sausage."

Why did he have to be so sweet? His charm was hard to resist.

The smell of the sandwiches made her stomach growl. Apparently, he really did watch what he ate. Even last night, he'd had a side salad with his grilled chicken, making her feel naughty by inhaling the beef sub.

"No breakfast sandwich for me?" Holden asked with a teasing grin. "I am letting you guys use the sheriff's office."

Neither she nor Sawyer smiled in response or looked away from one another.

"You always eat at home since you and Grace got married." Sawyer sipped his coffee, not taking his sad eyes off her, doing his best to make her squirm.

But it didn't work. She never let a colleague get under her skin.

Holden shrugged. "The gesture would've been nice."

"I'm not hungry. You can have mine," she said flatly, holding Sawyer's gaze, no matter how uncomfortable it made her with the air backing up in her lungs. "Thanks for the coffee."

Sawyer grabbed both sandwiches and tossed them, one at a time, sinking each into the trash bin without even looking. "You want to let your blood sugar drop. Fine. Neither of us will eat."

"Hey. Why are you wasting perfectly good food? Do you know what Mom would say?" Holden went to the bin and fished them out. "Ashley, are you hungry?"

"Actually, since I came in so early, I skipped breakfast. I'd like one," the deputy said, and Liz regretted not offering it to her.

"Bacon or sausage?" Holden asked.

"Sausage please."

He handed it to her. "I'll have the other for a midmorning snack." His gaze bounced from Liz to his brother. "This energy is different from last night. What is going on between you two this morning?" he asked, picking up on the tension that thickened the air.

"Nothing," she said, not letting any emotion leak into her voice or show on her face.

"On that we can agree," Sawyer grumbled.

She was thankful he didn't elaborate. There was a time when the two brothers spilled their guts to each other. No topic or detail off limits. Maybe Russo's presence stopped him.

Liz couldn't get over the injured expression on Sawyer, and warning clanged in her head, reminding her that wild animals were more aggressive, more dangerous when wounded.

Not that he should be the one upset. She'd only asked to wait to hash everything out until after they finished the case. Not for a reckless one-off kiss in her kitchen that dredged up in excruciating clarity everything she'd missed the past fifteen years. Aroused by pressing against that solid wall of muscle he called a chest. Teased by tasting him. Tormented by wanting to do it again. *Thank you very much.*

"Why don't we each take a stack of photos," Holden suggested. "If you can't ID the person, set it in the middle of the desk, and someone else will take a crack at it."

Everyone grabbed a chair. Russo dug into the sandwich with gusto, and before she finished, Holden had started on his second breakfast. The yummy aroma had Liz wondering if she'd made the right choice.

Deputy Russo needed it more than me.

They worked for a couple of hours, getting most of the names, discussing any contentious history between individuals that might be relevant when she came across a picture that gave her chills. White male. Late twenties. Brown eyes. Dark hair. Grinning like it was Christmas morning. The smile on his lips was subtle, but the gleam in his big bright eyes gave her pause.

Putting her coffee cup down, she held up the picture. "Who is this?"

Holden stared at the photo. "I know this guy. His name is on the tip of my tongue." He snapped his fingers, trying to think. "Released three or four months ago."

Tapping the photo, Liz said, "I bet he's a firebug."

Russo slipped in behind the computer. "I'm on it." She clacked away, typing for a few minutes. "Found him. Isaac Quincy. Convicted arsonist. Released three months ago."

"Can I take a look at the file?" Liz asked, and Russo moved aside. She skimmed through it. "According to his record, he has been in and out of jail since he was sixteen. Every arrest was for arson. Accelerants used were gasoline, kerosene and lighter fluid." She reviewed each incident. "Hmm. The fires escalated in aggression. His last two stints in jail were for burning down his childhood home while his parents were on vacation. He had been house-sitting. In the parents' statement, they said he was a 'good boy' who simply couldn't control himself. Mom didn't want to press charges. Dad did for his son's own good. The last one was for torching a dumpster while a homeless person was inside of it. Quincy claimed he didn't know the man was asleep inside. The victim suffered second-degree burns. No fatalities."

"Do you think he could be our guy?" Sawyer asked.

"It's possible." She looked around the room at the others. "He fits the profile, but these recent fires feel—"

"Personal," Sawyer said, finishing her sentence. "He didn't just set fires. He blew up the restaurant and turned the Compassionate Hearts into an inferno."

She nodded. "Not the work of a random firebug. But his recent release from prison coinciding with serial arson can't be dismissed, either."

"Maybe he was hired," Holden suggested, "by Kade Carver. I can't see him getting his hands dirty. I spoke to a couple of owners of other shops in those two blocks. They were reluctant to sell before, but after the fires, they've decided to accept Carver's offer."

"Deputy Russo, could you dig into it?" Liz asked. "See if there's any possible connection between Quincy and Carver. Find a thread, no matter how thin, we'll pull it and see where it leads."

"Sure." Russo left the office.

"I've been thinking we should set up a hotline for any tips," Liz said.

Holden frowned, not liking the idea. "Requires manpower to sort through all the crank calls we'll get."

That was a definite con. She was more concerned with the pros. "Can you spare it?"

"Will it be worth it?" he countered.

Sawyer sat back in his chair. "Do you really think we'll get a viable lead from a hotline?"

"No, I don't. I'm not going to hold my breath waiting to hear from a witness."

Holden sighed. "Then why bother?"

"Serial arsonists enjoy manipulating authorities. They like to communicate, explain themselves."

"You're hoping he'll call," Sawyer said.

She nodded. "We should check in with the medical examiner. See if we can get a time of death for Mike Steward."

"Easier to squeeze details out of Roger Norris in person. He doesn't like to talk over the phone." Sawyer stood. "It's a ten-minute walk."

Fresh air would be good. She needed to stretch her legs. "Let's go."

Neither of them initiated conversation along the way, which was for the best. He appeared resigned and she appreciated it. Maybe he'd gotten the message and would simply focus on the job. Something in her gut, though, told her not to cling to false hope since the air of misery hanging around him troubled her.

In the medical examiner's office, Roger Norris wore narrow rectangular glasses and his white lab coat over a gray AC/DC T-shirt with orange lettering. His thin dishwater blond hair was slicked back. His attention was focused on one of his many screens while he noshed on a banana.

Her stomach rumbled, and she wished she had eaten the breakfast sandwich instead of refusing out of anger. Or principle. If she had accepted the coffee, why not the food, too?

It made no sense, but Sawyer had her spinning in circles.

Roger nodded when they came in. "Sawyer Powell walks into my joint yet again. Can't stay away from me these days, can you?"

"Unfortunately not. This is—"

"Liz Kelley. I read your flattering quotes about the fire marshal in the *Gazette* today."

It was good of Egan to print it. She hoped her comments would change public opinion about Sawyer. "What can you tell us about Mike Steward?" Liz asked.

"Oh, plenty. Found something quite interesting." He scooted on his stool over to another screen. "His last meal was a burger, fries and a Coke. Based on his fractured skull, he was knocked out before his throat was cut. I got a lockdown on the estimated time of death. It was between four thirty and five thirty."

Nice and tight. That would be helpful.

"Was that the interesting part?" Sawyer asked.

"No, not at all. I'm getting to that. Saved the best part for last." Norris brought up something on his screen. A picture of a small typed note. "Found that stuffed in the victim's mouth toward the back of the throat."

It read, *SINS OF THE FATHER*.

"Any prints?" Sawyer asked.

Norris shook his head. "The perp was careful."

"Our guy wants to talk to us," Liz said. Just like she thought. "We've got to persuade Holden to dedicate manpower for a hotline."

"Consider it done." Sawyer glanced at her. "The only question is what sins did Neil Steward commit?"

Chapter Nine

The awkward silence between Sawyer and Liz, when they weren't discussing something pertinent to the case, unsettled him. She made it look easy, shutting off her emotions, staying laser-focused on work while he was struggling.

Back in the sheriff's office, Holden agreed to the hotline without protest after learning about the note the killer had left inside Mike Steward's mouth. By the time they'd eaten lunch, not a word exchanged between them, it was up and running.

"The *Gazette* and local news station will spread the word about the hotline. Everyone will know about it. We'll weed through the garbage," Holden said. "I'll only bother you with any tips that might be legit or if the perp calls in."

"Thanks," Sawyer said to his brother while keeping his gaze on Liz. Not that it seemed to faze her at all.

"I think Carver is here." She hiked her chin toward the hall.

Two men in business suits had entered the Sheriff's department.

Holden glanced over his shoulder. "Yep. That's him and his lawyer."

She shoved back from the desk and got up. "I can do the interview alone if you'd rather not do it together," she said, her voice flat.

"This is my case." He wiped his hands and crumpled up

the wrapper from lunch, throwing it away. "You're welcome to join in the interrogation room. If you can handle it."

"I don't see why I wouldn't be able to. There's nothing personal about this for me."

Her rejection earlier was like a knife in the gut, and here she was twisting it. "You've made that clear. We can talk to them in interrogation room one."

She pulled on a phony professional smile. "I'd like to question him here in the office instead."

"Why?" Sawyer asked.

"It'll make him less defensive. He might let something slip since he'll be less guarded."

Sawyer nodded. "Fine with me."

"I'll show him in," Holden offered.

"If you don't mind, I'll do it." She headed for the door. "Believe it or not, I'm good at putting suspects at ease."

Watching Liz walk away down the hall, Sawyer wanted this *wound*, deep in his heart, to scab over, to scar and fade. Instead, it festered and hurt. Infected by the past.

Holden turned to Sawyer. "Why is Liz acting like a robot? Her voice is all monotone and her eyes are blank. And you threw away food earlier. Fess up. What happened?"

Sawyer watched her greet Carver and his lawyer with a plastic grin. "I happened. I kissed her this morning."

"Well, that's a good thing, right?"

He glanced at his brother out of the corner of his eye. "Based on what you've observed thus far, does it look like it was a good thing?"

"Sorry." Holden folded his arms across his chest. "You've waited fifteen years for this. What's the plan?"

Liz said something that made Carver grin and look down at his suit with pride before he ran a hand through his white hair.

"There is no plan. All she wants to do is give me the

Heisman or run away from me." Each time it was like being kicked in the teeth. "She doesn't want me."

What if their time together had been lightning in a bottle? Not meant to last or not meant for them to have a second chance.

Then he thought of her pressed against him. The way she'd tightened her arms around him in the hug, sighed like she wanted more. Kissed him back. No restraint. Full of desire like she *did* want him.

"Maybe it's not you she doesn't want," Holden said. "Maybe she just doesn't want to get hurt."

"But I'd never hurt her."

"She might not be so sure of that."

Sawyer glanced back down the hall. He noticed Liz tugging up her neckerchief as she had a deputy get two cups of coffee for Carver and his lawyer.

What she'd said to him in the kitchen came back to him. How she'd never get married and have kids and that he knew why.

His heart sank at the thought of her denying herself the kind of life she wanted because of the scars. The accident had never mattered to him, but it still mattered to her. Perhaps in a way he couldn't fully understand.

Holden put a hand on Sawyer's shoulder. "Remember that basketball game you finished with a broken foot sophomore year?" his brother asked.

It had hurt like hell. "Yeah, of course." He'd never forget it.

"Any other player would've stayed off that foot. Avoided putting any pressure on it. Human nature to protect yourself from what's going to hurt. But not you, because you don't quit," Holden said. "No matter how painful, no matter the consequences, you don't give up when you're going after something you want. Your Liz is back in town. You can't quit now. Stop moping like a puppy that lost its home. Remember what you are."

Liz started escorting them over.

"And what's that?"

"A coyote," Holden said, referring to their high school mascot. His brother howled low enough for only them to hear and then crossed the hall to his office and closed the door.

The pep talk lifted his spirits. Holden was good at that. In fifteen years, Sawyer hadn't given up hope. Today, he had not only held Liz, but he got to kiss her, and for a moment it was everything.

Progress.

Only a coward or a fool would quit now. Sawyer was neither.

He grabbed an extra chair and brought it around behind the desk. Liz ushered them into the office. The two older men sat across from the desk.

Sawyer took the seat near the computer.

"Once again," Liz said, sitting beside him, "we appreciate you taking the time out of your busy schedule to come down here."

"Of course. I'm happy to help." The fifty-five-year-old man took a sip of his coffee, gagged and set the mug on the desk. "I just don't know how I can."

"We understand you're interested in purchasing all the businesses between Second and Third Street from Kern Avenue to Sycamore Road," Sawyer said.

"I am. It's to build a townhome community in the town center." Carver folded his hands in his lap. "Part of a housing growth plan I've coordinated with the mayor."

"Would you say you're hands-on with your businesses?" Sawyer asked. "That you're aware of details."

With a nod, Kade Carver grinned. "Certainly. It's how I

became so successful. I even know the name of every tenant. The devil is in the details."

"Have you had any holdouts who have refused to sell?" Sawyer asked.

"A few."

"Chuck Parrot recently invested a lot to renovate his restaurant." Liz's tone was soft, casual. "Was he interested in selling?"

Clearing his throat, Kade Carver narrowed his eyes. "He overextended himself with the loans he took out for the renovation. He was having trouble making the payments, so he was considering my offer."

"What about the nail salon?" Sawyer sipped his coffee that had been delivered with lunch.

Carver's mouth twitched. "We were in negotiations for a price we both felt was fair until the fire."

"Did Mr. Steward, the owner of the tattoo parlor, indicate he was interested in selling?" Liz asked.

Carver's gaze slid over her. "I'm not exactly sure where this line of questioning is leading. Are you accusing me of something?"

Smiling, Liz shook her head. "Sir, you are not being charged with a crime. Can you answer the question?"

His lawyer leaned over and whispered in his ear.

"No, the Stewards didn't want to sell," Carver said. "At first. But like any good businessman, I got to the root of their hesitation and came up with a viable solution. I assured them I would find them a suitable replacement location, which was the sticking point. Neil agreed to sell his place if he liked the alternate site. Otherwise, no deal. Seemed fair to me. I wasn't worried about it. They have a cult following and a reputation that'd ensure the business would thrive regardless of where it was moved. Or at least it did."

"The recent fires have lowered the property value of the businesses located on the two blocks you're interested in purchasing." Sawyer let that hang in the air for a moment. "Isn't that correct?"

The man shifted in his seat, looking a tad uncomfortable, but his lawyer saved him from responding. "My client hasn't had a chance to thoroughly review how the fires have affected the value."

"I hope you don't think I'm running around town torching these places," Carver said. "I may be a cutthroat businessman, but I am no killer. And why would I burn down a cabin? Or Compassionate Hearts? Huh?"

"To throw off the investigation," Sawyer said pointedly. "To keep the trail from leading to you. It's called misdirection."

Carver puffed up his chest, his cheeks growing pink. "I was at home last night. With my wife."

Liz nodded. "Of course you were. I'm certain she'll verify."

"She will indeed. And when the cabin was burned down and those hunters were murdered," Carver continued, "I wasn't even in the state. I was in Florida. With my wife."

"Mr. Carver," Liz said, holding up a gentle hand, "we don't think you doused any of these places in an accelerant and lit the match."

The man gave a smug grin. "I should hope not."

Leaning forward, Sawyer rested his forearms on the desk. "But it is entirely possible that you paid someone to do the dirty work for you," he said, and Kade's jaw dropped. "You're the only person who would financially benefit from any of these fires. Mr. Parrot swears you're behind it."

"Chuck Parrot is a drunk and a liar." Carver's tone turned vicious. "Only a fool would listen to him."

"This interview is over." The lawyer set his coffee mug

down and stood, prompting Carver to do the same. "We've cooperated and graciously answered your questions. Unless you charge my client with a crime, he has nothing else to say. Good day."

"Mayor Schroeder is going to hear about this." Carver wagged a finger at them. "Trying to pin this on an innocent businessman because you can't do your job."

The lawyer beckoned his client to hurry along. As they stalked out of the office, they ran into Neil Steward, who was coming into the department.

Mr. Steward marched up to them, shaking a fist in Carver's direction. "If you're behind this, like Chuck is saying, if you're the reason my boy is dead, I'll kill you." The deputy at the front desk jumped up and got between them. "Hear me? I'll kill you!"

"Thank you for threatening my client, not only in a room full of witnesses, Mr. Steward, but also law enforcement. Should any harm come to him, they know who to arrest." The lawyer steered Kade Carver out of the department.

"What do you think?" Sawyer asked Liz.

She glanced at him, and he could see the wheels turning in her head. "I hate it when loved ones are used as alibis because it can be hard to get to the truth, but it's a lot of people to kill just for profit."

"More have been killed over less."

She nodded. "Unfortunately, that's true. The restaurant was the first fire set. Then the nail salon. The cabin and the thrift store could be about misdirection."

Neil Steward was headed their way.

"I hate the type of conversation we're about to have with a grieving parent," she said.

"Me too." It was the hardest part of the job.

"I'd never given it much thought before, how fire marshals

also have to do this." The first glimmer of emotion flickered in her green eyes.

They stood as Neil Steward walked into the office. In his midforties, he was a burly guy, full mountain man beard, tattoos covering his exposed arms.

"I'm Agent Kelley and this is Fire Marshal Powell. We're sorry for your loss. You have our deepest sympathies." Liz shook his hand. "Please have a seat. Is your wife joining us?"

With bloodshot eyes, he dropped down into a chair. "She's too distraught to get out of the bed."

Understandable. They had just lost their only child.

"Can we get you a coffee?" she asked, and he shook his head. "We understand you received a threatening phone call right before the fire started."

"Sure did. Some weird guy. Said I deserved what was about to happen. 'Fireworks.' That was the word he used. I thought it was a buddy of mine messing around, but then he said he was going to take my boy and my shop."

Sawyer exchanged a look with Liz. "Did he say why he believed you deserved it? Have you crossed anyone that you can think of?"

Scratching his beard, Neil thought about it. "No, no, he didn't give me a reason. I just assumed the guy was a whacko. He was talking bananas. My wild days are long behind me. I don't make trouble with anybody. You can ask my wife. She'll tell you."

"May we see your phone?" Liz held out her hand. After he unlocked it and placed it in her palm, she looked through his calls. "Is this it? At ten thirty-five?"

The grieving father nodded. "Yeah. That's the one."

"From the exchange, it looks like it's from a disposable phone. A burner." Liz wrote the number down along with how long the call lasted. "Did you recognize the voice?"

Another shake of his head.

"Are you sure the guy didn't say anything else? I only ask because one minute and forty-five seconds is a long time." More had been said, Sawyer was certain of it.

Neil glanced around the room, once again thinking. "No. He, um, repeated it a few times. Yeah." He scratched his beard. "Wanted to make sure I got the message."

"Fireworks, he was going to take your son and your shop because you deserved it, but no reason was given. That's all?" Sawyer asked, wanting to be clear, and Neil nodded. "Do the words *Sins of the father* mean anything to you?"

Neil swallowed convulsively, his Adam's apple bobbing in his thick neck as his eyes turned glassy. "No," he said in a pained whisper. "Should it?"

It was plain to see that it did. Why not share everything he knew to help them catch this killer? What was he hiding?

"When was the last time you spoke with your son?" Liz asked.

"Sometime earlier. Before dinner. It's in there." He pointed to his phone.

Mike's name came up a little after four.

That confirmed the estimated time of death the ME had given them, between 4:30 p.m. and 5:30 p.m. "What did you two discuss?"

"Not much." Neil shrugged. "Someone had called him earlier and made a same-day appointment for that night. Mike planned to be in the shop for five to six hours."

Liz made a note. "Did he say who the appointment was with?"

"A guy who requested Mike. Insisted on having privacy and didn't want a bunch of other tattoo artists gawking at him. He wanted a really intricate tattoo on his chest of Vulcan, the god of…" His voice trailed off.

"Fire." Sawyer got up and came around the desk, sitting beside him. When Neil raised his head, with tears brimming in his eyes, Sawyer put a comforting hand on his forearm.

"The sicko who killed my boy and burned the place to the ground made an appointment?" Horror filled his face.

"It's our understanding the shop's hours varied." Liz's tone softened. "The only way to ensure Mike was the tattoo artist available at a specific time was to make an appointment."

Neil dropped his head into his hands and sobbed. "Do you think the murderer made Mike give him the tattoo before he killed him? If so, that's how you could find him. Right? Look for the tattoo."

"No. I don't believe he actually got a tattoo from Mike." Liz clasped her hands on the desk. "The killer wouldn't want to linger any longer than absolutely necessary."

There were no CCTV cameras near the front of tattoo parlor to capture the person going in around the time in question. "Did you have security cameras inside the shop?" Sawyer wondered. "With a backup downloaded to an online server?"

"No need. We don't keep cash in the shop. Debit or credit card only. Nothing inside a meth head would break in to steal. We've never had a problem. Until now."

"Did Mike live with you?" she asked, and Neil shook his head, tears leaking from the corners of his eyes. "Did he usually call when he was done for the night? Maybe after he locked up?"

"No, we didn't keep tabs on him like that. He was twenty-three. Did his own thing. We spoke to him once a day. Sometimes every other day."

"Mr. Steward, did you agree to sell your tattoo parlor to Kade Carver under the right terms?" Sawyer asked.

"I was willing to consider it." Neil sniffled. "If he found a new location that I liked. The offer, the money was pretty good. Evelyn, my wife, wanted me to take it. Mike didn't care either way."

Sawyer glanced at her to see if she had any more questions.

She shook her head. "Mr. Steward, if you can think of anything else, perhaps, if more details about the phone call come back to you, please don't hesitate to contact us." She handed him her card.

"You have to catch whoever did this." Neil stood and trudged out of the office.

Watching him pass the front desk, Sawyer turned to her. "You think he's holding back about the phone call, too?"

"A hundred percent. Whatever was said might be the key to helping us find the killer, but for some reason he's not sharing."

Deputy Russo made a beeline to the office. "There's a connection between Kade Carver and Isaac Quincy. Kade owns an apartment complex. Four buildings. One hundred units in total. Quincy is one of his tenants."

"Good work." Liz flashed a genuine smile.

"Carver is into details. Claims to know the names of all his tenants. He'd also know that Quincy has a record, and it would be easy enough to find out he's got a penchant for playing with fire," Sawyer said. "It can be hard for a convicted felon to reintegrate in society. Get a job. Maybe Carver offered him money or free rent to start the fires."

"Only one way to find out." Liz stood. "You got an address?"

Russo held up a piece of paper.

"Thanks." Sawyer took it from her, and the deputy left. "Are we riding separately or together?" he asked Liz.

"I didn't realize you were going to give me a choice."

He grabbed his cowboy hat from the side table and put it

on. "That's the thing, Liz. You decide for both of us. It's always been about your choices." He could've kicked himself for going there. He hadn't meant to; the words had just slipped out and there was no taking them back.

A blank expression fell over her face like a mask, and the distance between them grew without either of them moving.

After holding his gaze, without responding for so long, tempting him to speak first, she finally breezed past him and out into the hall. The clipped pace of her steps all business. No seductive sway of her hips, no grace. A formidable stride that he loved.

He hurried to catch up.

"One car," she said flatly over her shoulder, not looking at him. "It's more efficient."

She was something else, and man, did he love her.

Chapter Ten

After the quiet car ride, where they each stayed in their respective corners, Liz let Sawyer take the lead at Quincy's third-floor apartment.

He approached the front door and knocked. Hard. "Isaac Quincy. LFD and FBI. Open up."

Movement came from inside, a shuffling sound and then hurried footsteps, but not toward the door. Metal creaked. "Fire escape?"

"He's running." Sawyer drew his weapon and kicked in the door, busting the frame. Glock at the ready, he swept inside.

Pulling her sidearm, Liz followed behind him.

The window at the back of the living room was wide open. She caught a glimpse of the top of Quincy's head as he pounded down the steps.

Sawyer darted through the living room and ducked out the window. Liz was right behind him.

Lifting his head, Quincy glanced at them with a panicked look and clattered down the first flight. The fire escape led to the roof of a smaller adjacent building. Quincy leaped over the metal railing, landed on the smooth blacktop, slipped once and took off.

Liz swore under her breath. "Quincy, stop!"

Sawyer hopped the railing with the skill of a gymnast

over a pommel horse, but when his feet touched down, he clutched his injured side with a groan.

With little effort, she made it over the railing and kicked it into high gear. Sawyer chased him. Liz followed.

They ran across the rooftop. At the edge, Quincy jumped to the next building, making the six-foot leap, but dropped to his knees.

"Sawyer! Stitches!" she called out, not wanting him to aggravate or reopen his wound from absorbing the shock of the landing.

He halted at the ledge, either listening to her or using caution, and raised his weapon, taking aim. "Freeze, Quincy. Or I'll shoot."

The man dared to get up and take off running again.

Holstering her sidearm, Liz lengthened her stride, jumped to the next rooftop and landed in a tuck and roll. Then she popped up to her feet. "Stop!" she yelled.

But he didn't.

And neither did she.

Liz dashed after him and lunged, tackling Quincy, forcing him to his belly. She wrangled his arms behind his back and slipped on handcuffs. "Now we're going to chat down at the station instead of your apartment."

STARING THROUGH THE one-way glass of the observation room in the sheriff's department, Liz studied Isaac Quincy and considered how to play the interrogation.

Sawyer was standing in the back of the room, silently plotting how to throw her off guard, no doubt. She could feel his gaze on her, burning a hole in her backside.

"You were impressive back there." Sawyer came up beside her. "You jump from rooftops a lot?"

"Not every day." She glanced at him. "How is your side?"

"Sore, but I'm good." One corner of his mouth hitched up in a half smile.

Maybe it was the irresistible look he gave her or the adrenaline still pumping in her system that made her want to caress his cheek. Whatever the reason, she put it in check. "Are there any smokers out there?" She gestured to the bullpen.

"I think there are a couple. Why?"

Without answering, she headed out to the main area of the station. "Who has a lighter I can borrow?"

The deputy manning the front desk stood. He dug into his pocket, pulled out a Zippo and tossed it to her.

Catching it, she said, "Thanks." She dropped it in the pocket of her FBI jacket that she was still wearing and turned to Sawyer. "Let's go question him."

They headed down the hall. He opened the door for her.

She went in first, taking a seat at the metal table across from Quincy. The young man was pale and lean. A bit sweaty, which was to be expected after he ran. Wary brown eyes. Dark hair.

Sawyer pulled out the chair next to hers, making it scrape across the floor.

Straightening, Quincy began to fidget.

Liz met his nervous gaze. "We want to talk to you about the recent string of fires."

"I didn't start any of those fires." He spoke, using his hands in an animated way. His tone was immediately defensive. "I swear, I'm innocent."

"Of course you are." Sawyer leaned back in his chair. "That's why you were doing wind sprints across the roof, forcing us to chase you."

Perspiration beaded Quincy's forehead. He was anxious, but his eyes were angry. "I'm just tired of being harassed every time someone lights a match in this town."

"You're a convicted arsonist." Liz eyed him. "It's routine for us to question you when something like this happens."

"I did my time." Quincy put his elbows on the table, his expression turning indignant. "I got treatment inside. I'm rehabilitated. Ask my parole officer. Better yet, ask my court-appointed therapist."

"Oh yeah?" Liz wished she had a dollar for every time she heard that one. "So you don't get off on fires at all anymore?"

"That's right." He gave her a smug smile.

She reached into her pocket and slowly pulled out the Zippo. Watched Quincy's gaze drop to it. She fiddled with the metal lighter, turning it in her hand while he stayed transfixed. Flipping it open, she made him wait a few seconds before letting him see the flame.

Wrapping his arms around his stomach, he tried to look away, once, twice, and failed.

Liz snapped the lid of the lighter closed and watched the disappointment cross his face. "Want another?" She already knew the answer.

He nodded like a junkie in need of a fix.

She gave it to him. Holding the Zippo at eye level, even closer to Quincy's face, she struck the flint wheel, producing a flame. "Tell me about the Cowboy Way shop fire."

Licking his lips, Quincy smiled. "Perfection. It was a thing of flipping beauty." His eyes glazed over with that same Christmas-morning look. "In full swing by the time the fire department showed up."

Sawyer crossed his arms. "You admit to being there?"

"Well, I was at the grocery store two blocks away. Smelled the smoke. Had to follow it, and I found that glorious sight. So, yeah, I watched it. Along with half the town. No crime in that, or are you going to lock up everyone who was there?"

"Not everyone." Sawyer shook his head. "Only the fire-bug with a record."

"What did you think of the other fires?" Liz waved the flame. "Were those beautiful, too?"

Quincy shrugged with his gaze on the lighter. "I didn't see them. I was working the night the restaurant and the nail salon burned down. No reason for me to go to Bison Ridge."

"What about the inferno at Compassionate Hearts?" Warily, Sawyer studied him. "I'm sure you didn't miss that one."

"Wish I'd seen it, from what I heard on the news, but when I got off work, I went straight to bed. The fire happened sometime later while I was asleep."

Not unusual for him to keep track of the fires. "Where do you work?" She closed the lighter.

"Night shift. Road work. We're repaving Route 130." Quincy rattled off the name and number of his supervisor.

"Has Kade Carver ever asked you to work for him?" Sawyer asked. "In exchange for money or free rent?"

Confusion furrowed Quincy's brow. "Mr. Carver? No."

"What about any of Mr. Carver's employees?" Sawyer followed up.

The young man shook his head.

"Have you ever set a fire for someone else?" She put the lighter in her pocket. "For money?"

Quincy snickered. "That's not why I do it."

No, it wasn't. "Please answer."

"Never."

"Hard to believe," Sawyer said, "considering the way you looked at that lighter. Like a man willing to set a fire for any reason at all."

"You don't know me. You cops are all the same. I want a lawyer. Or I want out of here right now."

"You're free to go." Liz gestured to the door, and Sawyer gave her a side-eyed glance.

Isaac Quincy didn't waste a second scurrying out of the room.

"What are you doing?" Sawyer sighed. "We didn't even verify his alibi."

"He admitted to being at the Cowboy Way fire without him knowing we already had proof he was there. Quincy talked about it like he was admiring someone else's work. Not his own." She shifted in the chair, facing him. "It's natural for him to follow the other fires in the news, to remember when they happened. His alibi will check out."

"Don't tell me you believe he's rehabilitated."

Standing, she headed for the door. "Not at all. It's only a matter of time before he sets another fire. When he does, it won't be for someone else and certainly not for money."

They walked together down the hall.

"Some arsonists are paid," he said.

"True." She stopped in the doorway of the sheriff's office and leaned against the jamb. "But not Isaac Quincy. He's a pyromaniac."

He rested his shoulder on the other side of the door across from her, standing close. Intimately close. "That's exactly my point."

She could feel the heat radiating from his body. "I came here after giving a presentation at a symposium. During my seminar, I asked the participants—fire agency personnel, law enforcement, even a few insurance investigators—what was the definition of pyromania? Not a single one got it entirely right. Pyros deliberately set fires more than once. Showing tension or oftentimes arousal before the act. They are fascinated and attracted not only to fire but also to its paraphernalia. They feel pleasure, a sense of relief when setting them.

But above all, they must also set fires for fire's sake. Not for money or revenge or attracting attention."

He hooked his thumb in his belt and leaned in. "Well, I guess I'll have to reread that chapter in your book." His minty breath brushed her face. "But if you're so sure Quincy is a pyro and not our guy, why did we haul him in for questioning?"

"I suspected earlier, but I wasn't sure until we had him in the interrogation room. Running didn't help him, either. The more I think about this, whoever is behind the fires isn't a professional arsonist providing a service or doing it for profit. This is way too personal. Especially with Mike Steward's throat being cut. Then calling Neil, luring him to the fire, making him watch."

"Revenge. For the sins of the father."

"Most adult arsonists who aren't for profit are almost always seeking revenge."

"If only we knew why Neil Steward 'deserved it,'" he said, using air quotes.

"Makes me wonder if the others 'deserved it,' too, in the mind of our perpetrator. Did Chuck Parrot say whether he got a call before the fire?"

"When I talked to him, his entire focus was on the substantial amount of money he'd just lost and the fact he was financially ruined. He didn't mention it, and I didn't know to ask at the time."

Someone came into the station, drawing her gaze. "Don't turn around."

Sawyer did exactly what she told him not to do. A string of curses flew from his lips. "Bill Schroeder."

The mayor beckoned to someone with a stiff hand, and Deputy Russo hurried over to talk to him.

Liz grabbed Sawyer's arm and tugged him into the office. "Do yourself a favor and let me do the talking."

He glanced down at where she was touching him. "You expect me to stay tight-lipped and simply accept whatever horse manure he decides to dump on me?"

She let him go. "You're angry with me, I know—"

"I'm not angry." He stepped toward her. "I'm hurt. Confused. Because you won't talk to me. Fifteen years of no returned calls or emails. Here we are standing in the same room together, and I still can't get any answers."

Something in his eyes squeezed at Liz's heart, and she had to batten down her emotions. If she could have the toughest conversation of her life while working on this case with him and not lose focus, she would, but even she had her limits. "After things settle down." She looked back at the bullpen, where Russo and Schroeder were still talking.

"We could've been killed by that car bomb yesterday," he said, drawing her attention squarely back to him. "Things never settle down. There's always something."

Looking irate, Bill Schroeder headed for the office.

"Right now, that something is the mayor." She took a deep breath, wishing he'd stop pushing, even though he made a valid point. "But there is one thing I can do for you."

"What?"

"Protect you." When this case was done, he had to live in this town. Mouthing off to the mayor would not make his life easier. "Let me."

With a reluctant nod, Sawyer went around the desk, sank into a chair and propped his boots on the corner as Bill Schroeder charged inside the office and slammed the door shut.

"Why on earth would you accuse an upstanding citizen from a good family such as Kade Carver of arson and murder?" he asked, staring at Sawyer like Liz didn't exist.

"Bill." Removing her FBI jacket, she took a tentative step toward him. "Liz Kelley. I don't know if you remember me."

He'd been ahead of them in school by a couple of years and had also been a teen camper at the Wild Horse Ranch, but his last summer had been the one prior to the fire.

Finally, he met her eyes. His scowl softened. "I remember you. I also know about your little book. You're supposed to be an expert. I shouldn't have to tell you that the guy doing this is probably some lowlife who comes from a broken, abusive home with a history of violence and couldn't possibly be Kade Carver."

"Mr. Carver wasn't accused or charged," she said. "Simply questioned as part of this investigation."

"When I was informed the FBI would be assisting with this case, I was relieved at first. But now I see why nothing is getting done," Bill said, with a sneer. "Are you here to work or to canoodle with your old boyfriend?"

Sawyer let out a withering breath, but without uttering a word, he took out his phone and lowered his head.

Clasping her hands in front of her, Liz held tightly to her composure. "I'm here in a strictly professional capacity. My colleague, who, even after an attempt was made on his life to impede this case and was injured, has been working tirelessly to see justice served."

Bill rolled his eyes. "Spare me the song and dance. Save it for the press. Apparently, Erica Egan is lapping it up. Great article in the *Gazette*, by the way. Really pulled at the heartstrings," he said sarcastically. "What I want to know is if you're both incompetent? I demanded an update from Deputy Russo. She informed me that you had a convicted arsonist in your custody as a suspect and released him."

"Because he didn't set these fires." She strained for calm. "Would you like us to arrest anyone who fits the profile regardless of innocence or guilt?"

"How about you arrest someone? That'd be nice. The longer this goes on, the worse it looks for me." Bill smoothed down the lapels of his suit. "My opponent is running a tough-on-crime campaign. I need to be tougher. Do you under-stand?"

She swallowed a sigh. The man only cared about himself and getting reelected. Some people never changed.

He and Sawyer were both from old money, the kind that came with influence and power. Bill's family made it from the Schroeder Farm and Ranch Enterprises, part of the larg-est distribution network of major suppliers of agricultural in-puts. Sawyer's family made it from the Shooting Star Ranch, one of the biggest in the Mountain West region. That's where the similarities between the two of them stopped.

"I can assure you, Bill, that what will not help us resolve this case any faster is you getting on television talking about the arsonist, giving him all the attention he craves. Less than twelve hours after your reckless appearance on a major news network, which only served to embolden the perpetrator, he burned down the Cowboy Way and killed Mike Steward."

"How dare you accuse me of making this situation worse," Bill said, fury giving his voice a razor-sharp edge. "As though exercising my first amendment right somehow encouraged him to strike again."

"If the cowboy boot fits," she said.

"I could have your badge. Do you know that?" Bill crossed the room, coming up to her. "One call to my daddy." He held up a single finger, his tone setting her teeth on edge. "He plays golf with the governor, who knows the attorney gen-eral. Your boss's boss," he said, now pointing in her face, and she was half tempted to break the digit that was an inch from her nose to teach Bill the consequences of bad manners.

Sawyer barked out a laugh. "Did you really pull the Daddy card?"

He had been doing so well being quiet. Of course, it couldn't last.

Bill's gaze snapped to Sawyer, fixing on him.

But she stepped in front of the mayor, redirecting his anger. "I suggest the only comments you have to the press about this case are 'No comment.' Let the professionals working on this speak to the media about the facts. My boss is SAC Ross Cho." She scrawled his number, including extension, on the back of one of her cards. "Give him a call, he'll tell you the same, and by all means, take your chances trying to get me fired." Her record spoke for itself. No one at the bureau was going to cave because an entitled man-child was having a tantrum.

"We'll see if you're untouchable, *Lucky Liz*," Bill said, and hearing the nickname sent a chill through her. "As for lover boy, if he doesn't solve this soon by putting someone behind bars or in a grave, I'll call a city council meeting and have his badge. You can bet your bottom dollar it won't be a game of chance then. That's a promise."

Bill waltzed out, leaving the door open and her exasperated.

"How did he get elected?" Spinning around, she waited for an answer from Sawyer.

"His daddy's money. Also, he puts on a good show at town hall meetings. Packs away his real personality and pretends to be someone pleasant."

"I forgot what he was like." She ran a finger under her scarf, longing to take it off. "How awful he could be."

Sawyer put his feet on the floor and sauntered over to her. "I didn't." He held up his phone, showing her what he'd been doing.

"You recorded the conversation?"

"Bet your bottom dollar I did," he said, imitating Bill.

She laughed, as he'd meant for her to.

"Let that schmuck call his council meeting." He smiled, his eyes glittering. "You did a great job drawing his fire away from me. Once again, impressive."

Fighting for him, having his back was nothing. She'd do anything for him. Sacrifice everything if it meant he'd be happy.

Snapshots of their teenage days together flickered through her head. Then she remembered something Bill had said. "Have you seen the *Gazette* today?"

Sawyer walked over to the side table, picked up a copy and quickly scanned it. When she tried to look, he pulled it away from her line of sight. "You don't want to see it."

Dread slithered down her spine. "Give me the gist."

"Egan dug." He grimaced. "She brought up the past. The fire. Us. All of it."

She cringed. This town was already overflowing with busybodies who delved into everyone's business for sport. Now her painful past had been rehashed as entertainment. It wasn't news.

Sawyer put a hand on her back and rubbed. She was tempted to accept the comfort, almost did, but she noticed everyone in the bullpen watching them.

Adjusting her scarf, she moved away, turning her back to the gawking deputies.

"Let's get back to work." He tossed the paper in the trash. "Instead of focusing on garbage."

He was right. She should've said it first.

"We need a lead. We're missing something with this case." But what?

Sitting behind the desk, she brought up on the computer screen the original pictures Russo had taken, not the zoomed in versions that focused on individuals, and looked them over, one after another. A sinking sensation formed in the pit of her stomach. Staring at the photos, she should've seen it sooner.

"What is it?" he asked. "You're thinking something dark."

"There's a possibility that we have to consider," she said, reluctantly. "Investigate to rule it out if nothing else."

His brow furrowed. "I'm not going to like this, judging by your tone, am I?"

She shook her head. He was going to hate it. "Some arsonists are firefighters."

"No," he snapped.

"Hear me out. It's a persistent phenomenon and a long-standing problem. Sometimes they suffer from hero syndrome, but I don't think that's the case here. It's clear this is about revenge."

"Not in my station," he said with a definitive shake of his head. "I know those people. Trained with them. Battled fires with them. No."

"Arsonists start early. Usually in their teens. If he was never caught and convicted, he could be flying under the radar. He's skilled. Knows how much accelerant to use, where to place it, the timer, the car bomb. It would be easy for him to hide in the department," she said, and he scrubbed a hand over his face. "We'd be looking for someone with a decreased ability to self-regulate. Might drink a little too much. Unlikely to succeed in relationships. Divorced. Never married. White male. Sixteen to thirty-five."

"That's half the station. Most are divorced or unmarried. Hell, I fit that profile."

"If there's a firefighter with a vendetta, who is using arson to kill his victims—"

"You're reaching. Yesterday, you thought this string of fires and murders might be related to what happened at the summer camp."

She took a deep breath, hating the unease worming through her over having been mistaken about the link to the summer camp. "We have a time of death. Let's question them to see where they were." Since all the fires had started using a timer, they had no way to pinpoint when the devices had been planted. Mike Steward's death, as horrific and senseless as it was, might be the only way to find the killer. "Verify alibis. Investigate those who don't have one. Rule them out as suspects, if nothing else, and move on." *Hopefully.*

His frown deepened as he raked his hands through his hair, considering it.

"Do you have a better idea?" she asked.

"We talk to Chuck Parrot again to see if anyone called him before the fire."

"That will take five minutes. Questioning all the firefighters in your station as well as the volunteers will take hours. Possibly days. And that's with help from the deputies that Holden can spare. We need to get the ball rolling tonight. We can do it at the fire station to minimize the inconvenience and impact. Chuck Parrot can swing by there. What do you say?"

He groaned. "The olive branch they extended to me, consider it kindling."

Chapter Eleven

In his office at the fire department, Sawyer sat on the sofa trying to prepare himself to do this. Question his own as though they might be guilty. It left a bad taste in his mouth.

Gareth took a seat in the chair opposite him and Liz. From his expression, he wasn't too happy about this either but had agreed to let them interview everyone currently on shift and had someone calling those who were off to see if they didn't mind swinging in tonight. Otherwise, they'd be expected to come in tomorrow.

"Thank you for letting us get started with this as soon as possible," Sawyer said.

Resting an ankle on his knee, Gareth settled back in the chair. "Don't thank me until after you've spoken with Ted," he said, his lips giving a wry twist.

Sawyer wasn't looking forward to it.

Liz picked up her pen and notebook, about to get started, when the alarm in the building clanged. "Just when I thought we'd get through the day without a fire."

Gareth was up on his feet, rushing for the door. "Let me find out what it is." In less than a minute, he was back, already pulling on his gear. "Not a fire. Bad accident on I-80. A fuel truck and three cars. Interviewing the team will have to wait until tomorrow. But one off-duty person showed up.

Tonight isn't a complete bust for you." Ducking out of the office, he waved at someone to go in and then was gone.

Tessa strutted inside, flashing a tentative smile. She was a slender woman with tempting curves on display in a form-fitting sundress pulled off the shoulders. The hem was only a few inches lower than her backside. She wore matching cowboy boots and makeup, lips a bold, daring shade of red. Her dark blond hair was all glossy curls, skimming her bare shoulders. And she smelled good, too.

There was no denying she was a beautiful woman or that his hormones recognized it, but his heart only beat for Liz.

"Gareth told me you had some questions for everyone," Tessa said, her gaze fixed on his, and flipped her hair over her shoulder, kicking up the scent of her sweet perfume.

Clearing her throat, Liz tensed. "We do. Please have a seat. We'll try to make it quick."

Tessa slipped into the chair and crossed her legs, flaunting a dangerous amount of skin.

"You were on duty yesterday?" Sawyer asked.

"Yep." Smiling, she swung her leg and drummed her red-painted fingernails on the arms of the chair.

He kept his gaze up above her neck. "Did you leave the station at any time while on duty?"

"Twice. To respond to the fire in the morning at Compassionate Hearts and later that night to respond to the fire at the Cowboy Way."

"You were here in the station between four thirty and five thirty, and someone can verify it?" Liz asked, staring down at her notepad, even though she wasn't taking any notes. She was clutching the pen so tight her knuckles whitened.

"I was. We had gotten up from a nap around three. Then a group of us played cards until dinner."

Liz jotted it down. "Who did you play cards with?" she

asked, and Tessa provided the names. "Then I think that's all we need from you."

"When I got here," Tessa said, "I was told I'm the only one coming in tonight," she said, and Sawyer wondered if her buddy Bridget was the one making the calls and had ensured no other off-duty personnel would show up.

He glanced at his watch and then at Liz. It was almost nine. "I guess we'll call it a night. It's late anyway." They could start fresh in the morning.

The three of them stood.

Tessa slinked up beside him and slid a hand up his arm, curling her fingers around his biceps. "Sawyer, can I speak to you privately?"

He turned to Liz, her face inscrutable, and then caught a flash of jealousy in her eyes. Or was it his imagination and he was seeing what he wanted?

"Take your time." Liz's voice was encouraging, even enthusiastic. She grabbed her things and headed for the door without looking back at him. "I'm going home. See you tomorrow," she said in a rush, disappearing out the door and shutting it behind her.

He gritted his teeth that they'd driven to the fire station separately to avoid the hassle of doubling back to pick her vehicle up later. He knew how this must appear to her and didn't want her leaving with the wrong idea. More importantly, he didn't want her at the house alone.

"Can we sit for a minute?" Tessa glanced at the sofa.

Sitting was how it would start. Then she'd climb onto his lap and lower his zipper. "I'll stay standing. What'd you need?"

"I know your heart and head is in the right place, but I don't think questioning everyone is going to go over well with the others," she said cautiously.

"There might be some tension for a few days, but once we catch this guy, it will all be worth it."

She moved closer, brushing her curves, the ones that could make a monk ache to touch her, against his body. "I know you said not tonight, but I'm free and you're free, and I could use the pleasure of your company." Running her hands up his chest, she wrapped her arms around his neck. "Let's go to my place and get dirty together." She moistened her lips. "Or we could lock the door and do it right here while everyone's out."

Many men would've loved to take what she was offering. He wasn't one of them.

Sawyer pulled her arms from around his neck and put lots of space between them. "Tessa, we won't be hooking up anymore." They hadn't for a while, not since she asked him if he ever wanted to get married and have kids and when would they start going out to dinner on a proper date? Alarm bells went off in his head, and that had been that for him. He had hoped they could've avoided the dreaded conversation. "It's not you. It's me."

"I scared you off, didn't I? I figured if I gave you a little time, a lot of space, you'd come back because you missed me."

He only thought of her when he saw her in passing and hadn't missed her, which was telling. But he didn't want to hurt her, either.

"I don't need things to get serious right now. I'm good just having fun. No strings attached," Tessa said, lying to him, possibly even lying to herself.

Putting his hands in his pockets, he edged farther back. "This isn't what I want."

"Tell me the truth. I know you've got needs, and one day you'll settle down."

"The truth is I want to get serious."

Her gaze flickered over his face as understanding dawned in her hurt eyes. "Just not with me."

He picked up his hat and put it on. "The right woman is back in my life. I can't lose her again."

"Liz."

Sawyer gave one firm nod.

"I got that feeling last night. When I pulled you to the side, you kept glancing over at her while we spoke. I had to give it one more shot."

"Did Bridget make sure no one else was coming in tonight?"

Biting her lower lip, she gave him a guilty smile.

"You're going to find the right guy," he said. "When you do, he's going to be lucky to have you."

Tessa sighed. "I got all dolled up for nothing. At least tell me I look nice."

"You look really nice."

"Thanks for being honest with me. I know plenty of guys who would've taken me up on my offer for a good time on that sofa and, once finished, would've chased after the woman he really wanted."

"I'm not that kind of guy." And Tessa deserved better.

She pressed a palm to his cheek. "Which makes this even harder. Because you're one of the good ones."

"I have to go."

"To chase after her?"

In a manner of speaking. "Yeah."

Confronting Liz about the past and getting answers he deserved was one thing. Knowing for certain whether she was still attracted to him, wanted him or cared for him was another story. The idea of her being afraid of getting hurt—by him—made something inside his chest crack open and bleed. And if that was the case, then he needed a different approach.

Liz finished brushing her teeth and slipped on her cotton pajama bottoms and tank top. Turning off the light, she couldn't stop thinking about Tessa, her svelte figure or the dress she wore, which left very, very little to the imagination.

Not that Sawyer needed to imagine. He'd already enjoyed Tessa Anderson's entire package.

He was probably doing it again right now.

Good for him.

Acid burned through her veins. She needed to finish this case and get back to Virginia.

A car pulled into the drive.

Grabbing her weapon, she jumped from the bed and crept to the window. She shifted the edge of the curtain to the side and peeked out.

It was a red Fire Department SUV. Liz checked the time. She'd only been home for thirty minutes. He must have turned Tessa down. Surely, no easy feat, considering the dress, the hair, the cowboy boots.

Relief and regret battled inside her. He deserved to act like it was business, or rather fun as usual, not restricting himself simply because she was in town. Soon enough, she'd be gone.

Sawyer climbed out of the vehicle and shut the door, but instead of traipsing off toward the trees, he was making a beeline for her front door.

Her pulse spiked.

As if he sensed her watching him, he looked right up at her window, straight at her through the silver of darkness where she hid. Then he disappeared under the porch.

The doorbell rang. Her chest tightened. It rang again. And again.

What did he want? It was late, she was exhausted, the lights were out, and the house was quiet. Obvious "do not disturb" signs.

He knocked at the door.

Maybe there was another fire or murder and rather than call, he wanted to tell her in person. She put her weapon on the nightstand beside the knife she wore strapped to her ankle, grabbed her long-sleeve pajama top, buttoned it and headed downstairs. As she made it to the first floor, the knocking turned into a fist pounding.

She opened the door and yawned like he had roused her from sleep. "What is it that couldn't wait until morning?"

"I had a question." He stepped across the threshold and stalked toward her.

Liz shuffled away, but he kept coming. She backed up until she had no place left to go. He didn't say a word as he placed his palms on the wall behind her, on either side of her head. He leaned in, and his mouth crushed hard on hers, making her breath catch and her legs turn to jelly. She didn't fight. Didn't pull away. The wind had been knocked out of her by the suddenness, the urgency under it, and the scorching need that slammed into her like a force of nature.

He was kissing her with a hot, focused intensity. She couldn't stop herself from kissing him back, drinking in the taste of him, slipping her fingers into his hair, bringing him even closer. A moan slid up her throat, and the next thing she knew, her mouth was free.

He'd taken a step back and stared down at her, studying her, assessing something.

"What are you looking at?" she asked, her voice shaky, fragile. She hated the sound.

"I've got my answer." Sawyer winked, spun on his heel and headed for the door. "Good night." He slammed the door closed.

Had he asked a question?

THE NEXT MORNING, Liz rolled over in bed and hit Snooze on her beeping alarm clock for the fourth time, which was unlike her. She usually forced herself to get up, threw on her clothes and went for a run. Today, she was physically, mentally and emotionally exhausted. Between the arsonist-murderer on the loose and Sawyer wearing her down, she'd earned the extra rest.

Last night, after he kissed her, leaving her lips swollen and awareness coursing through her body, she couldn't sleep for hours. She'd ached.

Ached to be touched.

Ached to be with him.

Still did.

Looking down at her bare arm on the side that was worse, she ran her fingers over the variation in shades and texture.

As a rookie, she'd tried to get intimate with a guy, a fellow agent. They'd met during the academy, became friends, flirted. She told him about the accident. Downplayed the scars. Why go into graphic detail? After graduation, he asked her out. Back at her apartment, she'd swallowed her fear and thrown caution to the wind following a couple of shots of whiskey. Once her shirt came off, their make-out session changed, the gleam in his eyes slid from desire to distaste.

The awkwardness lasted for a moment and an eternity. She fumbled to shut off the light, as if that'd make a difference. The sun eventually had to rise—no hiding forever. He uttered an excuse about forgetting something work-related and having to get up early. That was that.

Even though she had built a life, stitched herself up with so many missing pieces, to this day, she wondered if some holes could never be filled, some wounds never healed.

Staring at her arm, she was painfully aware of the stark difference between knowing a thing and seeing it. Touching it.

The ache inside swelled. Tears gathered in the corners of her eyes. She clenched her jaw against the loneliness closing in around her.

I'm fine. I'm fine.

A buzzing pulled her from her thoughts. She glanced at her phone and cringed. Was there another fire? Another victim?

This case was a mess of cruel death and fiery destruction.

Shaking off her self-pity, she answered the phone. "Agent Kelley."

"Hello, this is Nurse Tipton calling from Laramie Hospital. Mrs. Martinez didn't make it through the night. She's passed."

Sitting up, Liz shoved back the covers and put her bare feet on the worn wooden floor. "Thank you for letting me know." She clicked off.

The weight of another senseless death was heavy not only on her shoulders but also in her heart. They had to find this guy before he did more harm.

She rushed through a shower. Not bothering to blow-dry her hair, she brushed it thoroughly. She decided on slacks, a gray scarf with delicate blue polka dots, and light blue button-down.

In the kitchen, she made coffee as she stared out the window at the tent Sawyer had slept in again. She fired off a text to him about Aleida and got to work on whipping up a quick breakfast. She was at the stove scrambling egg whites and chopped up veggies with her back to the door when she heard him come in. The screen door snapped closed behind him.

"I'm sorry," he said. "About Aleida."

She didn't turn to look at him. Simply nodded.

He stood still a minute and then headed upstairs, and the shower started. She made a couple of breakfast burritos and, after leaving one for him on the table, took hers and coffee in a travel mug outside onto the porch.

She sat in one of the old rocking chairs and, though her appetite hadn't kicked in yet, munched on the food.

Her father had been a fourth-generation farmer. Their property—before they'd sold most of it to the Powells—reached up from the break land plateau to Big Horn Ridge. She loved the snowcapped rolling mountains, the brown and green hills, wide open space, clean air, the lack of congestion. The view helped put things in perspective, making it hard to deny the sense of loss inside, the gnawing emptiness that hollowed her out that had nothing to do with the case.

Not once in her career had she allowed her personal business to interfere with her job. Somehow, she had convinced herself it was due to the fact she was a good agent. Every time she looked at Sawyer, she questioned that conviction. Not her being a good agent part. Maybe it had been so easy for her to separate the personal from the professional because she'd never had anything else in her life before that she cared about.

And she did care for him. Deeply.

The screen door creaked as he stepped outside, shutting the front door. "I'm ready if you are."

Getting into his vehicle was her response. Sawyer drove while he ate. With her fingers laced together, hard, she stared out the window until they pulled up to the fire station on the side of the building where his office was located.

There was a long moment of silence, the only sound the running engine and AC blowing. Sawyer reached over and covered her hands with one of his palms. She hadn't realized how cold she was until his warmth penetrated.

A knock on the driver's side window drew their attention, and he moved his hand. Erica Egan stood on the other side wearing a skintight tank top, bent over, with an enviable amount of cleavage on display. She held up a tray with three coffees and flashed a pearly white smile. "Time to chat."

As Sawyer groaned, they both got out of the car.

He slammed the door shut. "After the last article, no more quotes." He headed for the door to the building.

Wearing khaki shorts and heels that showed off her long, taut legs, she click-clacked ahead of them and threw herself in front of the door. "We had a deal."

Liz's gaze swept over Erica, her bare arms, smooth legs— her effortless sex appeal. It made Liz wonder why she hadn't ever appreciated the curve of her neck when she was younger, the smoothness of its skin. How she had even taken for granted her pale freckles.

She tugged on the neckerchief.

"You brought up painful things that should've been left in the past and out of the *Gazette*." Sawyer crossed his arms. "Things that have no bearing on this case."

"I beg to differ," Erica said. "You two have history, and I picked up on a certain vibe between you, which might affect how you handle the investigation."

"What you picked up on was that I'm not interested in letting you sidle up to me for information." He reached for the door handle.

The journalist blocked him. "I framed both of you in a positive light and used the entirety of Agent Kelley's glowing quote about you."

Erica offered Liz a coffee cup. She accepted it, though she wouldn't drink it. Paranoia prevented her from consuming food and beverages from strangers. Not that she thought the reporter was going to poison her. She simply couldn't do it, but accepting the coffee was a gesture of good will.

"I also did as you asked," Erica continued. "No vivid descriptions of the fire. I painted the perpetrator as a monster and highlighted not only the loss of two parents but also the awful impact on the entire community."

"You read the article, Sawyer." Liz glanced at him. "Did she?"

By the tightening of his jaw, Erica had. "Nothing else about the fire fifteen years ago or describing Liz as the girl who survived. Agreed?"

Grinning, Erica handed him a cup.

He took the peace offering.

"A source told me you are changing the focus of your investigation to the firefighters, as you may suspect one of them is the culprit. Can you confirm or deny?"

How did she find out so quickly? Sawyer had to call Gareth, who in turn called Ted, last night to set up the interviews for all personnel today, but word had traveled much faster than either of them had expected.

"Who told you?" Sawyer asked. "And don't give me any hogwash about confidential sources."

"I overheard a couple of firefighters griping about it at the bar last night. Beyond that I can't reveal my sources. Is it true?"

"We have to examine every possibility," Liz said. "Today we're only conducting routine interviews. We thank the fine men and women of the LFD and VFD for their cooperation and appreciate their invaluable service to the community."

"Have a good day, Ms. Egan." Sawyer grabbed the handle and opened the door, letting Liz inside first. Once the door closed on the reporter, he said, "Holden and his deputies will be here soon to help out."

"It's going to be a long day." Probably grueling. "Are you ready for this? For their skepticism. For the hostility." She'd been in this situation before—questioning firefighters—and what she'd faced was nothing short of vitriol.

"Does it matter if I'm ready? We have a job to do."

Chapter Twelve

"This is unbelievable," Ted Rapke said, sitting in a chair in Sawyer's office, his face rigid with tension. "You actually think it's one of us?"

"I don't." Sawyer's head was throbbing after going through this for hours. The same questions, similar responses, different firefighters. "But it's necessary."

Scooting to the edge of the sofa beside him, Liz rested her forearms on her thighs. "Please answer the question. Where were you between four thirty and five thirty last night?"

Ted sighed. "I left my shift early. Around three. Three-thirty. I met my fiancée, Cathy, and was with her the rest of the night."

"I'm sure she'll verify." Liz gave a tight smile. "Why did you leave early?"

"We recently got engaged. I haven't given her much input on the engagement party. Telling her whatever she wanted was fine with me apparently wasn't good enough. Her mom was coming into town this morning, and she wanted to go over things the night before. Put on a good show. You know? Gareth agreed to cover for me."

"Has your relationship been rocky?" she asked.

Ted's gaze swung to Sawyer and then back to Liz. "What has that got to do with anything?"

Sawyer gritted his teeth, hating to subject the guys to this. "She needs to form a complete profile of everyone."

"Not per se." Ted rubbed his hands up and down his thighs. "I've been married twice before. I want to make this one work."

"What time did you meet her and where?" Liz opened a bottle of water and took a sip.

Ted shrugged. "Maybe four. At her place."

"Do we have enough?" Irritation ticked through Sawyer.

Liz sat back and crossed her legs. "Sure. We'll need to contact your fiancée, but that's all for now."

"You know we've all been through a background check. We risk our lives every day to save people. It's one thing to question us, dragging us in on our day off, or asking us to lose sleep, but you shouldn't put the volunteers through the wringer." He pushed to his feet, with disgust stamped on his face. "Their numbers dwindle every year."

"One more question," Liz said. "You know everyone in the department and the volunteers very well."

Ted narrowed his eyes at her. "That's a statement, not a question, but yeah, I do."

"Do you have any rock stars? Someone who can't get enough of the job, works extra shifts, a volunteer who joined young and is at every single call, at the front of every work detail."

Ted's face hardened. "You should be ashamed of yourself, Liz. Now you want to go after someone who's dedicated and earnest. Is this a joke? What kind of investigation are you running?"

"Sadly, this is no joke." Liz stood. "At least one hundred arsonists who are also firefighters are convicted every year. In North America alone. That's only the ones who've been caught. If this arsonist is a firefighter, then 'earnest' is precisely who we are looking for, because beneath that layer of dedication is a need for self-importance. It's the type we go after when a serial arsonist is running around, and frequently enough, there's good reason."

Waving a dismissive hand at her, Ted walked out of the office.

Sawyer jumped to his feet and went after him. "Hold up," he said, and Ted stopped but didn't turn around. He hurried around to face him. "I don't like this any more than you do. The goal is to eliminate everyone in the LFD and VFD as suspects. But if this guy is hiding somewhere in our ranks, it's unacceptable. One thing we take pride in is our integrity and the trust that the community has in us. If one of our own is an arsonist and a murderer, he's everything we detest."

The words gave Ted pause, deflating the anger in his face. Slowly, he nodded. "You're right, but that's still a mighty big *if*."

A door across the hall from them opened. Holden and Joshua Burfield stepped out and shook hands.

Ted walked away, heading over to Josh. "Want to get out of here and grab a quick drink before I have to explain to my future mother-in-law why we're being questioned?"

"Sure, let's get Gareth," Josh said. "Hey, have you set a date for the engagement party?"

After this, Sawyer doubted an invitation was in the cards for him.

"Not yet." Ted gave a weary shake of his head. "Can't agree on a venue. I don't want to spend as much money on this party as we will on a wedding."

Holden followed Sawyer back into his office and closed the door.

"How's it going?" Liz asked.

"So far, most everyone we've questioned have had alibis."

"Let me guess." Liz sighed. "Thirty percent were here on duty. The rest were with loved ones."

Holden put his finger on his nose. "Bingo. Girlfriend, fiancée, brother, mother. I'll have a deputy verify them all."

"We have a list, too," Liz said. "At the top of ours is Ted Rapke. We need solid times from the fiancée."

Sawyer bristled. Ted could be aggravating and hold a grudge. That didn't make him a murderer and an arsonist.

"I've also got two we have to look into deeper," Holden said. "Alibis are weak."

"Who?" Sawyer sat down.

"Gareth McCreary. He wasn't on duty at the time in question because he was getting ready to fill in for Ted. States he went to the grocery store on Third to pick up stuff to cook dinner for the company, paid cash and can't find the receipt. Arrived at the station at five. Someone else said he didn't arrive until five thirty. We'll check the surveillance cameras at the grocery store to see when he was there."

"The store is only two blocks from the Cowboy Way." It had been a quick walk for Isaac Quincy.

"The other person?" Liz asked.

"Johnson, the probie."

Sawyer recalled seeing him at the fire. "But he was on duty."

"He was, but he left the station earlier that day to run an errand. Picked up a prescription and pastries from Divine Treats."

Not good. Wincing, Sawyer scratched the stubble on his jaw. He needed to shave. "The pastry shop is around the corner from the tattoo parlor."

Liz stretched her neck and adjusted her scarf. "What time?"

"He was gone from five to six. It'll be easy to establish exactly when he picked up the prescription. Divine Treats is a different story. There are no cameras inside or at the traffic lights on the block. We'll check with the stores across the street. I think there's even an ATM, too."

"Sounds good." Liz finished her water. "If we can't clear McCreary and the probie, let's see if they'll agree to take a polygraph test."

"All right. One more thing. Josh Burfield couldn't convince all the volunteers to come in for questioning. Two took it as an offense. One quit. I'll talk to them personally tomorrow." Holden yawned, and exhaustion was starting to set in for Sawyer, too. "It's getting late. I'm cutting my deputies loose, but I'll stick around a few more hours to help you question the next team on the way in. Best to push through what we can tonight." His cell phone buzzed. He answered it. "Chief Deputy Powell." While he listened, his gaze slid to him and then Liz. "Okay. Wait a sec. I'm going to put you on speaker." As he did so, he said to them, "We got something on the hotline Russo thinks you need to hear." He moved closer. "Go ahead and play it, Ashley."

"This came in a few hours ago, but we just now got to it because we've been inundated with worthless calls and phony tips. Here you go."

The message played. "You think I'm a monster. I'm anything but." The voice was deep and sinister. Electronically modified. "I am vengeance, making them reap what they have sown. Ask them how they built their businesses, where they got the seed money. And they will lie. Ask what they're hiding. And they will lie. I took a son for the sins of the father. Did he tell you about our chat? Did he tell you why he has been punished? Or did he lie? I have taken everything from two, leaving them their lives and their lies as their cross to bear. Fire was my weapon. My anger, my hatred, was best turned into a flammable fuel. Because it's effective and nothing burns as clean."

"That's the end of it," Russo said. "We're trying to trace where the call came from."

Sawyer swallowed around the thick knot in his throat. "I thought I'd be relieved if he left a message," he said, feeling the complete opposite. "Like we'd get a clue, or he'd tip his hand, and we'd see some way to stop him."

"Can you play it again?" Liz asked. The second time they listened to it, she took notes. "Russo, we're going to speak to Parrot today. Can you contact Neil Steward and ask where he got the money to open the tattoo parlor? The same with Aleida Martinez's husband. He might be able to fill in some blanks for us."

"I'm on it."

Holden disconnected.

"He may not have left us a clue," Liz said, "but he gave us a way to find one. It's getting Steward to tell us what he's hiding."

"Maybe Parrot will be more forthcoming," Sawyer said, hoping for the best but expecting more lies. Neil had lost his son and his shop, and still he was determined to protect his secret.

A deputy poked his head into the office. "I've got another firefighter for you to question."

"I'll take him," Holden said, moving to the door.

Sawyer glanced at his watch. It was only five, but it felt much later. "Thanks, Holden."

"No problem." His brother gave a two-finger salute. "Here to serve." He left the office.

"It almost sounded like our guy was finished." Sawyer grabbed a bottle of water. "The way he used the past tense."

"Possibly. It's been two days with no fires. No car bombs.

No murders." She stared at her notes. "But part of it was also in present tense. I *am* vengeance. *Making* them reap what they have sown. He was careful with the way he worded it for a reason. His type gets a thrill out of manipulating law enforcement."

"I hope he's done and that there are no others he intends to punish. But he does want us to find out what Steward and Parrot are lying about. Perhaps that's part of his plan. How he gets to us. If it's illegal, then we'll finish the punishment."

"That's what they do. Manipulate while reminding us that he's in charge. Even if he is finished with his vendetta, we're not going to let him get away with murder and arson." Resting her head on the back of the sofa, she pinched the bridge of her nose and closed her eyes. "We need a break in this case. What if you're right and we're wasting time conducting these interviews?" She heaved a shuddery breath. "What am I missing?"

"I never said it was a waste of time. I don't want to believe someone I know, I trust and I've worked with is capable of something like this. Have your instincts been wrong before on other cases?"

Her lashes lifted. "No, but—" she tilted her head toward him "—being back here is messing with my head."

She neglected to mention whether he was having any effect on her heart. He didn't want to be a distraction. Something to avoid. He wanted to be a safe place for her to fall when she needed it. He wanted to be there for her in every way.

Sawyer took her hand in his and the minute their skin touched sparks fired through his whole body. He rubbed the tendons along her inner wrist, a careless caress. Or maybe a careful one. He wasn't sure, but when she didn't pull away, he was starting to think that if he wore her down bit by bit, she'd eventually stop running. Talk to him.

"What's your plan tonight?" she asked.

"What do you mean?"

"Where do you intend to sleep? I hope it's at home in your bed and not in the tent again. You need a good night's rest."

Still rubbing her wrist, he stretched his torso until a twinge in his side made him stop. "I'm touched you care, even though you keep denying it."

"If you're tired, you're not going to be at your best during this investigation."

Leaning back, he angled toward her so that their thighs touched. "I see. You're only concerned about my job performance."

"That's not what I meant." Her voice softened.

Sawyer brushed hair away from her face, trailing his fingertips along her cheek to her chin and let it linger there. That was the thing about Liz. She always made him want to get closer. Always pulled him in, without even trying. "Care to clarify?"

A charged silence bloomed between them. She stared at him, her eyes pale green pools of warmth and uncertainty. All he wanted was to erase her doubt. About herself and him.

"I don't want to repeat the past," he admitted. "I know you've said you can't, but you need to know that I can't stop trying because I've never stopped loving you."

Her lips parted, her eyes going wide.

A sharp rap on the open door had them pulling apart. Chuck Parrot entered. "I guess the *Gazette* got it right about you two."

The last thing Sawyer wanted was for anyone to mention the article again.

Liz's shoulders tensed. "What do you mean?" she asked, and Sawyer was grateful she didn't know all the details in the article.

Parrot schlepped in—his thinning red hair wild and wiry as though he hadn't combed it—and plopped down in a chair like he'd been drinking or hadn't stopped in days. "Erica Egan wrote that you two had been lovers years ago until tragedy separated you and that this case has rekindled your connection."

The reporter had swapped one sensational focus for another. "Egan only cares about seeing her byline beneath the front-page headline."

"Doesn't mean she's wrong." Chuck pulled a flask from his back pocket.

"You'll have to wait," Sawyer said, "until we're done here to resume drinking."

Flattening his mouth in a thin line, Chuck sagged in his seat but kept hold of the flask, resting it on his round belly. "Well, hurry up so I can get back to drowning my sorrows." He shook the metal container.

Sawyer glanced at Liz to see how she wanted to handle it. She intensely eyed Parrot like a puzzle she wanted to piece together. So he got to the point. "Did you receive a threatening phone call shortly before your restaurant was burned down?"

The question sobered him quickly. He straightened, his eyes turning alert. "Excuse me?"

Sawyer waited for a beat, studying him. "Did someone call you minutes before the fire and threaten you?"

Chuck hesitated, and Sawyer could see the deliberation on his face. "No. No one called me. Why do you ask?"

"Because someone called Neil Steward right before the Cowboy Way was torched," Sawyer said. "Threatened to take away his son and his shop."

His gaze bounced around as Chuck lowered his head. "Did the man say why he was going to do that to Neil?"

"I never said it was a man who called Neil."

Chuck opened the flask and took a sip. "Merely assumed."

"I know you from somewhere," Liz said. "Don't I? Your face, your voice, very familiar."

"I don't think so. Maybe I have one of those faces. People seem to think they know me for some reason."

The round shape. Freckles. Pale complexion. Orange-red hair. His face was distinctive. Chuck was forty-two, ten years their senior, though he looked older, so Liz didn't know him from school.

"It'll come to me. In the meantime, may we see your cell phone?" she asked.

His brows drew together, and he moved his hand, covering his pocket that had the bulge of his phone. "No, you may not."

"Withholding information or evidence in a criminal investigation is obstruction of justice." Her tone was soft.

"I'm the victim here. You might want to remember that."

"Don't you want to help us catch this guy?" Sawyer asked.

"Yeah," Chuck spat out, nodding, "of course."

Sawyer cocked his head to the side. "Then tell us about the phone call."

"I would." Chuck stood. "But I didn't get one." He headed for the door.

"CP," Liz called out, and Parrot spun around. "That's what everyone called you on the Wild Horse Ranch."

He didn't say anything, his face turning ghostly white.

"It took me some time to recognize you. Easier here in the light of the office. You've put on weight. Your hair has thinned. Aged quite a bit. But you worked there my first year." She rose and edged toward him. "As a ranch hand, but you weren't there the next summer when the fire that killed the Durbins happened, right?"

Chuck shrugged. "Sure. So what?"

"Why did you say I didn't know you?"

Another shrug from him. "Guess I didn't make the connection. I don't recall every stinking kid that passed through there. Why? Is that a crime, too?"

He was a bad liar. Chuck Parrot had already admitted to reading the article in the *Gazette*. The Wild Horse Ranch fire had been mentioned. Even if he didn't remember Liz, he was aware of the connection.

Liz smiled in that practiced saccharine way Sawyer recognized. "Did Neil work there around the same time as you?"

Chuck turned the flask up to his mouth, taking another hit. Probably stalling. "You'll have to ask him about his previous work history."

"Where did you get the seed money to open your restaurant?" she asked.

Chuck's brow furrowed, and he rocked back on his heels like the question had been a physical blow. "Wh-what difference does it make?"

Maybe all the difference in the world.

"Where?" she pressed.

He rubbed his hand over the back of his neck. "Loan from the bank."

Ask and they'll lie.

Why?

"Which bank gave a ranch hand a five-figure loan to open a restaurant with nothing for collateral?"

Sawyer loved watching Liz work. She was sexy as she closed in, throwing razor-sharp questions to get at the truth. Not to mention seeing her chase down a suspect had been oddly thrilling.

"You don't know me or what I had to use as collateral," Chuck said defensively. "Frankly, it's none of your business. What should be is finding the sick SOB who took everything away from me. Is there anything else?"

She shook her head and followed him to the doorway, where she watched him leave. "How much do you want to bet Neil worked there, too?"

"It was a popular place. The Durbins hired many ranch hands over the years, and they were the only camp within a hundred miles that catered to older teens."

She cast a glance at Sawyer over her shoulder. "You still don't think there's something there, at the very least, something about the Wild Horse Ranch, rather than the fire, is the connection?"

"I'm not saying that." He was playing Devil's advocate. Statistically, this was more than coincidence. "We've got to look at it from all angles. Test the theory."

"I wonder if any records from the ranch still exist."

"The fire wiped out the main house and the cabins. The property was sold. Everything leveled. The Durbins didn't have any kids who we could speak with. But I do think there's something there." He came up alongside her. "Chuck knows you, but he lied about it because he didn't want us to associate him with the ranch. He also lied about not getting a threatening phone call and where he got his seed money for the restaurant. For whatever reason, Chuck and Neil are hiding the same thing. If we can figure out what it is, the connection will be solid."

"It'll have to wait." She gestured down the hall.

The next team of firefighters had arrived to be questioned.

Chapter Thirteen

He had enjoyed calling into the hotline, airing his grievance, giving his retribution a voice. Now others would wonder about the dirty deeds of those on his list. What he didn't enjoy was Liz's meddling. Yet again. He thought he'd be able to savor making her suffer, taking Sawyer away while she was forced to watch and dealing with her later in Virginia.

Turns out, she was a sharper agent than he'd assumed and should have given her more credit. She and Sawyer were asking all the right questions to all the right people, circling like sharks, getting closer than he could allow, smelling blood in the water.

Somehow, they had even corrupted the lovely Erica Egan. In the *Gazette*, she lauded Kelley and Powell for their efforts in the investigation. Baited readers to root for the star-crossed lovers on their journey to prevail as they rekindled a connection. It made him want to gag. All the while, Egan failed to describe the glory of his handiwork. Instead, she labeled those who had sold their souls to the devil as innocent victims. Called him a monster!

When he was only seeking justice.

Removing Liz Kelley and Sawyer Powell from the playing field was the safest answer to his growing problem. Then the reporter would revert to her old style—he was helping sell more papers—and he didn't need those two meddlers to ruin his game. After all, he had a spectacular finale planned. Something no one expected. Something no one could stop once it started. Something the likes of which no one in the Mountain West had ever seen. He was going to finish with a big *boom*.

More pain and suffering and fire was necessary. The greater the effort, the grander the gesture, the sweeter the reward. In the end, he'd get what he wanted, what he needed, and all the patience he'd shown, the risks he had taken, all the blood he had shed, would be worth it.

But first, he needed Liz and Sawyer out of the way. No more underestimating them.

He watched the cursed lovebirds slide into the red SUV that was parked right in view of the surveillance camera. He hadn't been able to get anywhere close to it. The inconvenience only forced him to improvise.

Regrettably, he wouldn't be able to take care of those two himself tonight. In case something went wrong, he needed an airtight alibi that was above reproach. For this one, he needed assistance. Someone he trusted.

Liz's luck was finally about to run out. She and Sawyer were completely unaware of what lay ahead and how their night would end.

SAWYER HAD TOLD her that he still loved her. Liz didn't know if that was possible. Or healthy. Or best for him.

That was all she could think about on the nerve-wracking drive back to Bison Ridge. Maybe he wouldn't bring it up tonight. Let them get some sleep and tackle it tomorrow.

She glanced at her cell. It was on ten percent power. She needed to grab her phone charger from the rental.

Sawyer pulled up behind her vehicle, which was in front of the house, and put the SUV in Park.

"I don't know about you, but I'm exhausted." She hopped out. "Good night," she said, closing the door.

He was right behind her. "Are we going to talk about it?" His voice was dark and deep and rumbly.

No. "Tomorrow. Okay?" She headed for the rental. "I'm beat."

She wasn't up to handling Sawyer. Not tonight. He'd always been able to see right through the mask she tried to wear to hide her emotions. Training had made her better, but still, he had that way about him. Like he could see her soul. The last thing she wanted was for him to glimpse her weakness.

"I told you I love you."

She faltered to a stop, her stomach tightening in a knot. "I know."

He put a hand on her shoulder and turned her around to face him. "I deserve a response," he said, gentling his tone, making it soft as cotton. Then he waited and waited. "Give me something, Lizzie," he said, the only one she ever allowed to use the nickname.

"Thank you." The two clumsy words tumbled from her mouth.

Sawyer shook his head as if he hadn't heard her correctly. "Thank you?" He reared back, pulling his hands from her shoulders. "Thank you," he snapped. "Tell me you don't love me. Tell me what you felt died a long time ago. Tell me that you don't want me the way I want you. Or tell me that you *do* love me. But don't say 'thank you.'"

Steeling herself, she looked at him, meeting his darkening stare, concealing the agony roiling inside her. "I don't want you to sleep in the tent tonight. Call Tessa. Give her a real chance. You might be more compatible than you realize."

He nudged the tip of his black cowboy hat up with his knuckle. "You're still trying to decide for both of us. As though what I want isn't a factor in this equation. You've gotten too accustomed to acting stoic, running away from anything that makes you feel something. No boyfriend. No husband. No friends. No pet. What about your family? All you've got is that badge and a gun when you deserve a hell of a lot more to fill the empty spaces in your life."

"You're one to talk. Where's your girlfriend or wife or pet?" she asked, skipping over the friends and family part since he had her there. "Who are you to judge me?"

"I noticed you neglected to address how you keep making unilateral decisions that affect both our lives. I'm done letting you kick me to the side with no explanation. You want to know why?" he asked, but he didn't wait for her to answer. "I am not a puppy, who'll slink away and lick his wounds. I'm a coyote." He started howling.

At her.

What in the world? Had he lost his mind?

Color rose in her cheeks. The only proof he was getting to her, making her feel something.

"Please," she said, "stop howling like some wild thing."

He howled again, this time even louder, letting out his frustration and his misery.

She heaved out a breath. "You have no right to make unfounded assumptions about my life," she said, raising her voice over his howls. "I have a great job. I'm proud to be an agent. To have a purpose." She glowered at him.

There she went, bringing up work as a deflection, so he kept on howling.

"I've built a good life and I'm perfectly f…" Her voice trailed off as she caught herself, something dawning in her eyes.

"What? You're perfectly *fine*?"

He must have struck a chord. She narrowed her eyes, lips thinning, spun around and opened the door to her rental car.

"I appreciate your concern, but go home." Her tone was weary. She reached inside the car and grabbed something. "This day has pushed us to our breaking point. You need to get some sleep. We both do."

Go home. He should do as she asked and let her be, but something inside him demanded he stay. This was where they needed to be, at their breaking point, so they could have a breakthrough.

She slammed the car door, holding a phone charger, and turned toward the house.

But he was right on her, closing the distance. He gripped her arms, making her face him. "Every good memory I have is tied up with you." His heart thudded in his chest.

Tears glistened in her eyes. "Then it's time to make good memories with someone new."

"Do you ever think about us?"

Her bottom lip trembled. "I try not to," she said, her voice breaking right along with his heart.

"I think about you every single day." Though his nights were the hardest. Yes, he'd had other lovers, but being with them only made him miss her more. When he was alone in his bed with only his memories for comfort, his regrets tortured him. "I've loved you for so long that I don't remember what it's like not to."

He'd let her run away before, but this time, things would be different. This time, he would fight for her and not give up.

A vehicle approaching, the engine a loud growl, had him pivoting toward the sound. A black motorcycle came down the road way too fast for the speed limit. Alarm pulsed through him. The person was wearing all black, a helmet covering his face. Sawyer had a split second of recognition as the motorcycle slowed, moonlight bouncing off steel. A gun.

An icy wave of fear rushed over him.

"Sawyer!"

Liz's voice barely registered as instinct kicked in. He whirled her away from the line of fire, and then they were both on the ground with his body covering hers, pain flaring in his side as a shot cracked the air.

The window where they had been standing shattered. Glass rained down on them. Thunder from more gunshots breaking windows in the house. He pressed her flat to the ground as another shot punctured a tire. He drew his weapon. A third bullet pinged off the frame only centimeters from his head, close enough to feel biting heat. He shifted even lower.

The motorcycle sped away, gunning the engine, tires screeching, leaving the odor of burnt rubber in the air.

Sawyer lay there, his body fully covering hers, one arm curled around her head, his face buried in her hair. He waited for a fourth shot that never came. They were gone. For now. He strained to hear if the vehicle had turned around and was coming back. Or perhaps stopped down the road and the gunman was on foot.

It would have been reckless, not to mention foolish, for the person to get off the motorcycle or give them a chance to catch the license plate. Then again, their assailant shot at an FBI agent in front of her house, so how wise could he be?

Sawyer's shoulder had taken the brunt of the fall when they'd landed. Her right arm was beneath him, her Glock looking heavy in her small hand. She'd drawn her weapon as he'd pulled her down, and he'd done likewise. "Are you hit? Injured?"

"No, but you're smothering me. Does that count?" She pushed his chest and he moved.

"I'm going to go after him." Anger burned along his nerves. This had gone too far. Liz could've been hurt. Or worse killed. Before he could get up from the ground, she caught his arm.

"You were shot. You're bleeding." She touched his forehead.

It stung. "Just a scratch. The bullet grazed me." He hadn't even realized how close he'd come to getting shot in the head. "He's getting away."

Still, she held on to him, worry heavy in her eyes. "He's already gone. Made it to the fork in the road by now. We can't be sure which way he went, and the motorcycle gives him off-road options. We are not splitting up."

Was that all it took, nearly taking a bullet for her to see reason?

"We'll call it in, and I'll get you cleaned up." She holstered her weapon and found her phone.

"You're not staying here."

"This is my house. I won't be run off."

"It isn't safe. First the car bomb. Now this. We're going to the ranch." His voice brooked no argument. He would do anything to keep her safe.

She squeezed her eyes shut. "I don't think I can face your family, handle the hugs and kisses and questions—"

"I live in the apartment above the garage. No one has to know you're there, if you stay with me instead of a guest-room in the main house." There was also the B&B in town, but it was much more exposed, leaving their vehicles vulnerable. "You can have the bed and I'll take the sofa. Okay?"

He waited for more arguments and was ready with alternative solutions. No matter her response, she wasn't staying. He was going to make sure she was protected.

Reluctantly, she nodded. Her gaze flew back to the cut on

his head and she threw her arms around him in a tight hug. "I'm so glad you're alive."

So was he.

Glad they were both alive.

Chapter Fourteen

Liz was still shaken by the close call. Whoever had shot at them had gotten away without a trace. They didn't catch the license plate to have something substantial to go on.

The sheriffs in Laramie and Bison Ridge as well as the police in nearby Wayward Bluffs had patrols on the lookout for one man, wearing black, riding a black supersport bike. Neither she nor Sawyer had caught the make to narrow down the field of what they were looking for.

Sawyer pulled up to the wrought iron gates emblazoned with his family ranch's shooting star brand. He punched in the code and the massive gate swung open. They pulled through, taking the long, tree-lined driveway illuminated by LED lights, and a wave of memories assailed her. All good and warm but still hard to face.

The Powell ranch was something out of a fairy tale or a movie, and she had once thought this would be her home.

"Are you sure no one will know I'm here?"

"It'll be fine," he said. "With the hours I'm working on the case, no one is going to come out to the apartment. Trust me."

She did trust him. Always had.

They passed the enormous main house that even had wings. Ten bedrooms. Twelve bathrooms. Buck and Holly Powell loved their family and wanted to keep them close. They built the main house hoping to have weddings, host holiday celebrations and throw big birthdays there. Enough space for grandkids, extended family, in-laws and friends to stay. They were a loving, close-knit family. Buck and Holly wanted part of their legacy to be keeping it that way for generations.

Liz had not only appreciated their vision but had also shared it. Believing this was what her life with Sawyer would look like. That they would have been married here. Raised their kids on this ranch alongside their cousins.

He parked at the side of the garage near the outdoor staircase that led to the apartment. No one peeking out of a window in the house would be able to see her exit the vehicle.

She grabbed her laptop bag, he took her carry-on suitcase, they got out, and they hurried up the stairs. Quickly, he opened the unlocked door and ushered her inside.

After closing it, he flipped the lock and slipped on the chain. "Mom has a spare key. It's an extra precaution. She usually gives us plenty of space when we're in the grind. And Dad, well…" He shrugged.

Buck Powell preferred to have his children come to him, call him, let him know when he was needed. He was an antihelicopter parent to the extreme, while Holly was a mama bear who wanted her children to be happy, healthy and safe.

"I'll put your bag in the bedroom." He started toward the room at the far end with the double French doors.

The garage apartment had been an idea for Monty, not yet realized the last time she was on the Shooting Star Ranch.

On the opposite end of the spacious apartment was a kitchen equipped with the essentials, including an island large enough to eat on. White cabinets and black quartz countertops. She took in the place. Hardwood floors and large area rug defined the living room with a cognac-colored leather sofa and large television. The place was cozy and warm and tidy.

Following him through the living room, she stopped in front of the framed picture hanging on the wall—an eighteen-by-twenty-four-inch poster of her posing with a copy of her book. It was surreal.

"I'm sure all the ladies you bring here love to see this." She gestured to it like she was Vanna White on *Wheel of Fortune*.

"As a matter of fact, they tell me it's what they like best about my place."

Surely, they loved the bed with Sawyer naked in it the best. "Did you get it from the bookstore?"

"Yeah. It's the one your mom custom-made. She paid a pretty penny for shipping." He stepped closer, eyeing it before looking at her. "Seriously, I don't bring anyone here."

"Why not?"

"Too personal. The ranch is about family." He went to the bedroom and set her bag down. "To bring them here would mean I'm interested in a future with them."

Questions rushed through her mind, but to ask them would only lead to trouble. "Mind if I shower?" She followed him into the room in the back.

The king-size bed was made, complete with accent pillows. The apartment looked like something out of a magazine, only lived in. His mother must have decorated.

"You let me use yours. Feel free to use mine." He flashed a weary smile, his eyes warm and sincere.

She looked at the bandage on his forehead, thought about the stitches in his side and ached to hold him close. Pulling her gaze away, she unzipped her suitcase. "Bathroom?"

He pushed open the door to the en suite. "Right here."

She fished out her toiletry bag and hurried into the bathroom before she acted on an impulse she'd regret. "Thanks." She closed the door and turned on the light.

The tile and stonework were dark and sophisticated. Masculine. Yet, there was still an airy spa-like feel. In the daytime, the skylights must have provided plenty of natural light. The large shower had smooth stone flooring and two showerheads. She started one of them.

She didn't take long getting cleaned up and brushing her teeth. Once finished, she looked around the bathroom and realized in her haste, she'd forgotten to bring her pajamas.

No way was she going out with only a towel wrapped around her. Sawyer was sitting on that bed waiting to talk to her. She just knew it.

She grabbed his navy robe from the hook on the back of the door, pulled it on and hung up the towel. Tying the belt, she rubbed her fingers over the ultrasoft cotton, nuzzled her nose in the collar and inhaled the scent of him. The loss hit her all over again. The stark reminder of what was waiting for her in Virginia. An empty condo and a cold bed.

Beyond the door waited a man who would push with questions that she owed answers to.

You can't hide in here forever, and there's nowhere to run.

She opened the door and stepped out of the bathroom. Sitting on the bed, he lifted his head and his penetrating gaze locked on hers.

A breath shuddered out of her with a lump in her throat like a boulder. She shoved her hands in the pockets of the robe, faking casualness. "Hope you don't mind I put it on."

"Not at all." He pushed off the bed and came closer. "You look good wearing my things." He flashed a sinful grin that made her heart tumble over in her chest.

Averting her gaze, she caught sight of a copy of her book on the nightstand. She thought again about the poster hanging in the living room and something he'd said. Actually, a lot of things he'd said. "Tell me something."

He stopped less than a foot away, within arm's reach. "Anything."

"How did you know my mom spent a lot of money on shipping for the poster? How are you certain that I don't have a social life or get sweaty with someone sometimes or have a pet or anything besides work?" All true, but she hadn't shared those private, embarrassing details with him. The only thing he didn't seem to know was whether she'd been in the house the day he came to Montana. And the reason he didn't know was because her mother hadn't been home.

The grin slipped from his face. He scrubbed a hand through his hair. "Your mom and I have kept in touch."

Anger whispered through her. *My mother and Sawyer have been communicating behind my back.* "All these years? Keeping it a secret from me."

"When I was in Montana, your mom happened to be in town and saw the Missoula sheriff hauling me in to the station. She got me released, made sure no charges were pressed, took me to a diner and fed me. We talked for hours. She didn't want me to pull another stunt like that. I agreed on the condition that she'd tell me everything. Give me updates about you."

Although she didn't visit her parents and didn't encourage them to fly out to see her—far too busy with work—she confided in her mother, too much apparently, since the information was routinely shared with Sawyer. "How often?"

"We talk three or four times a week."

The frequency was staggering. More often than she talked to them. "About what? It can't just be about me." Not enough going on in her life.

"Quilting. Bridge. Hunting. My job. My parents. She knows

everything going on with my brothers. Your parents even came to Holden's wedding."

Her parents were invited when she wasn't? Not that she would've gone. Still, the sting of betrayal cut deep. "You had no right."

He sighed. "Lizzie, just because you cut me off, didn't mean I was ready to let go. You…you were my everything."

Her heart lurched. He had been her whole world, too. The first person she wanted to talk to about anything, good or bad. When they were together, everything felt possible because he was hers and she was his. Then the fire burned away the future they wanted, reducing it to ashes, but letting Sawyer go had been a different kind of devastation.

"I thought it would be easier if we didn't have any more contact." Her voice was a whisper.

"Easier for you maybe. But not for me. I loved you. With everything I am. I still wanted the future we had planned. Going to college together at SWU. Getting engaged after graduation. Married once we had settled into our careers. I didn't stop wanting a life with you because of the accident."

"We were silly kids. With preposterous plans. Your high school love isn't supposed to be your only one."

Yet he was hers. Not just her first but her only.

"Who says? Try telling that to my parents."

The ideal couple. High school sweethearts. Never had an off year to explore other romantic interests. Married for forty. Four kids. Unbearably affectionate. An impossible standard.

"I was there at your side every day as you recovered in the hospital. You lost twenty pounds in one week. I saw the pain. All your struggles. Tried to help you through recovery, but you slowly started shutting me out until you moved away and cut off all contact."

A jolt of sorrow sliced through her. "I was doing you a favor. I thought that I'd be the only one who would suffer."

He shook his head. "You took away my choice. Made a unilateral decision for both of us." His voice was rough. Ragged.

"You were supposed to move on with some pretty girl and live the life you were always meant to have. Just with someone else."

Sawyer grimaced. "How could I move on when you haven't?" he asked, his tone intimate, bare. "How could I fall for someone else when all I do is compare them to you and hate how they don't measure up?" Lowering his head, he blew out a long breath. "Were you there that day in Montana? Were you home? Did you hear me, screaming for you until I was breathless?"

Her throat closed. A fresh wave of pain flooded her, but the ache was in her heart. "I was."

"Why didn't you come out and talk to me?"

Tears welled, threatening to fall. "Because I didn't want to be without you. I would've looked into your eyes, fell into your arms and never let go."

"That was all I ever wanted." He ventured even closer. "Why didn't you?"

She shut her eyes. Hot tears rolled down her cheeks. "I was broken. I'd lost myself. Everything good and beautiful and strong was tied up in you." As though there was no Liz without Sawyer. Using him to fix what was fractured inside of her wouldn't have been right. Wouldn't have been healthy. "I had to let you go, so we could both be free. Even though it had killed me to do it." She looked up at him. "I had to heal, find a way out of the darkness and back into the light, alone. Eventually, I did, and it led me to the FBI." The bureau gave her a renewed sense of purpose.

"Then why are you still running from me?" he demanded, sounding bereft.

"You haven't seen it." A pang returned to her chest. "The scars. The skin grafts. What I look like."

Hurt flashed on his face. "Because you never gave me a chance."

"A chance? For what? To reject me?" Her back teeth clenched. "To stay with me out of obligation? Some twisted sense of loyalty. Or worse pity?" Burdening him with the expectation to love her after the fire had left her *damaged goods*. "Why drag out the inevitable part where you eventually wanted to move on and dumped me."

"Since you thought me leaving you was inevitable, you left me first. When all this time, you should've believed that *you* and *me* being together is what's inevitable."

"The fire *ruined* me." The only way he'd understand was to show him. Loosening the belt, she turned her back to him and shrugged off the top of the robe, letting it fall to her waist. Then she pulled her hair over one shoulder. "Nobody wants to look at this, much less touch it. Especially not..." A lover.

She trembled, baring herself to him, exposing the scars and grief she carried.

Her heart throbbed so hard it hurt until he wrapped his arms around her, bringing her against him, with his warm chest to her back. She nearly pulled away, the heat of his body was scorching, but she was tired of running from the one person she wanted to cling to.

"You are not ruined." He pressed his mouth to the nape of her neck, his breath sending a tingle down her spine.

Over the years, she'd imagined what it would be like to see him again, to hold him, to be held in return.

This was real. Not a memory. Not a fantasy she'd had a thousand times.

"You're a warrior who goes into battle against the worst of the worst." Kissing her softly, he trailed a path across her back. "You're brilliant and brave and beautiful. Even more so now. Not despite the scars. Simply beautiful, scars and all. And you're still the sexiest woman I've ever known."

Curling her hands around his forearms that were banded tight around her, she closed her eyes and reveled in his touch, in the sincerity in his voice, in the way he smelled, in how he accepted all that she was.

He brushed her shoulder with his lips and slipped a hand inside the robe, palm pressed to her stomach.

His warmth penetrated past the scars and muscle, deep into her bones. With Sawyer, she was exposed. Vulnerable.

And it frightened her.

But then he did something even more terrifying.

He untied the belt, letting the robe fall to the floor and turned her around. His gaze swept over her body and there was only tenderness in his eyes. *Appreciation.*

Looking back up at her, he cupped her jaw, running his fingers into her hair. "I love you, honey. So much." He pressed the sweetest kiss to her lips. "Still. Always."

She was smiling and crying and shivering at the same time. "I love you, too."

A devastating smile broke over his face, and her thoughts scattered. He crushed his mouth to hers, his lips full of desperation and hunger. She kissed him back hard, longing sliding into every stroke of her tongue against his, concentrating on the taste of him.

He shuffled them backward, somehow caressing her as he pulled his shirt over his head. Their lips parted for a breath.

Then his mouth claimed hers again, and they let out twin sighs of relief.

The years they'd been apart disappeared as if they'd always been and should always be together.

She unbuckled his belt, shoved down his pants and boxer briefs. A sigh escaped her. He was gorgeous. Everything about him sexy and strong.

"Do you want me to shower first?" He kicked off his boots, working his jeans off the rest of the way.

After fifteen years, she should be able to wait five more minutes. But she couldn't. "I need you right now. We'll shower after. Together. Put those two showerheads to good use."

"Then we can get dirty again."

She laughed as they tumbled onto the bed in a tangle. The delicious weight of him on top of her settled between her thighs, his hands exploring her body while she delighted in the feel of his skin and muscles and strength.

Her body relaxed and tensed with anticipation. "It's been a long time for me. I haven't done this since…you."

He stared down at her and smiled. "We can go slow. Start with me kissing every inch of you." He pressed his lips to the base of her throat, licked across her collarbone and nipped her shoulder, sending a shiver through her.

Although that sounded like a dream come true, she didn't want to slow down. She wanted to rush forward. With him. "Let's save slow for tomorrow morning."

He kissed her again, his mouth warm and demanding as his hand slid down between her legs. The need unleashed within her was immediate—too powerful to deny. So much emotion in his touch. Love and joy and hunger. She felt the same. Fear wouldn't hold her back any longer.

Clinging to each other, tangled together. Connected. She

thought needing him made her weak. Only now she saw their love made them stronger.

That need for him all-consuming. No restraint between them. Only intensity and heat and love.

This was everything.

She'd been running all this time from where she belonged. Where she was always meant to be.

They were inevitable.

Chapter Fifteen

Missed? How had his brother missed?

He never did like guns, in part because of the uncertainty. Is someone alive? Dead? Is the wound fatal?

And guns were too loud. Crude. Say nothing of the mess they caused. Unlike fire. That was a different beast. His animal of choice. Sophisticated when done right.

His brother thought Sawyer or Liz might have been injured, but he was certain they were alive. What if she called in more agents to assist with the case?

Even if she didn't, the sheriff's department was going to throw their full weight behind solving this case. Deputies were already conducting interviews to speed things along. This drive-by shooting was only going to fuel their efforts.

Then there was Sawyer. His protective instincts would put him in overdrive. That Powell would stop at nothing now.

At least his brother had removed the license plates from the motorcycle and evaded the roadblocks authorities had set up. No danger of them figuring out who they were.

Gritting his teeth, he groaned. He was under pressure to see this through. Instead of being able to draw this out, like he wanted, he needed to accelerate his timeline.

Somehow, someway he would finish the list. No better time than now to make it happen. Starting with Neil Steward and Chuck Parrot. No protective custody had been given to them. Neither man had provided the authorities with enough to warrant it, too busy hiding their precious secret. Liars until the end.

And I was smart enough to bait Liz and Sawyer into thinking I was finished.

Far from it.

In order for this to work, before the sun rose, he needed to make sure Steward and Parrot were dead.

SAWYER WOKE WITH light streaming in the windows and Liz nestled up against him. And it was perfect.

She was perfect. For him. He only wished they hadn't wasted so much time not being together, but he finally understood why she'd needed to recover and grow on her own without him. Saw how she'd suffered. How she'd sacrificed for him.

Last night as he held her close, she'd told him about the rookie agent who had made her question if any man would find her desirable. What a weak fool that guy was not to see she was gorgeous. His loss was Sawyer's gain.

Now Liz knew that he'd had other options and still only wanted her. There would be no fear of entrapment. Of obligation. Of resentment.

No doubt.

With open hearts, they were choosing this—to be together.

Liz snuggled closer, her leg between his thighs, nuzzling her mouth against the curve of his neck. "Good morning," she whispered, her voice throaty and sexy.

He tightened his arm around her. "How are you feeling?"

"A whole lot better than fine." She gave his shoulder a playful nip. "Amazing, actually." She ran her palm across his chest. "It was like riding a bike. You?"

Like he'd been living with one lung, barely able to breathe. Now? "Everything is right in the world with you back in my life." In his arms where she belonged. Sex had never been an issue for him. Intimacy had. She was the one woman he'd been truly intimate with, sharing his deepest secrets, his real self. "There's nothing like this." He caressed her face. "Like us."

"I'll never let go again," she promised.

"You better not." He wouldn't survive if she did. "And last night." He gave a low whistle and kissed her. "I thought it was mind-blowing before, but that was next level."

"You're full of it." She leaned up on her forearm. "You said it was mind-blowing with Tessa."

"No, I didn't. I spoke in generalities that could be applied to any relationship." He brushed hair from her face and tucked it behind her ear. Caressed her cheek. Cupped the side of her neck. Felt incredible for her not to cringe. "Chemistry and compatibility aren't the same. We have both. Marriage shouldn't be based on sex, even if it's mind-blowing. That's what Dad told me after I informed him that I was going to marry you one day."

Her brows pinched together. "I don't know if I should be flattered that you were referring to us when you said 'mind-blowing' or creeped out that your dad knew so much about our sex life."

He chuckled. "Some private things had slipped out in an argument we had. I wanted to marry you right after high school. He thought we were too young and believed I was confusing great sex with love. That's when I came up with the plan to do it after college. But the takeaway is you should be flattered."

There was a loud knock on the door, and Liz tensed. His front doorknob rattled, someone trying to get in.

Good thing he'd locked it.

She yanked the sheet up, covering herself. "I thought you said no one would come here."

"Sawyer!" Holden's voice was urgent. "Open up."

"One minute," he called out and turned to Liz. "Sorry. I forgot Holden and Monty drive past the garage on their way out of the ranch." He jumped up and shoved his legs into his jeans. Leaning over the bed, he gave her a quick kiss.

After closing the French doors to the bedroom, he hustled to the front door, slipped off the chain, flipped the dead bolt and opened it, but stood holding on to the knob and frame so his brother wouldn't cross the threshold. "Hey, what's up?"

"I was heading out, about to call you and spotted your car. I thought you were camping out at Liz's. What happened? Did she run off the whipped puppy?" His brother tousled Sawyer's hair, and Holden's gaze flew to his forehead. "And what happened to your head?"

After Liz had called in the shooting, the Bison Ridge sheriff had responded, coming out to the house to take their statement. Sawyer had asked the deputies in Laramie not to notify his brother because Sawyer wanted to explain himself.

"Why were you going to call me?" Sawyer asked, redirecting him.

"Are you going to let me in?" He stepped forward, but when Sawyer didn't budge, Holden narrowed his eyes. "Is she inside?" he asked in a whisper.

Thankful his brother was discreet for once in their lives, Sawyer gave a casual nod.

Holden gave a loud howl that made Sawyer's gut tighten with embarrassment. "Way to go Coyote." He patted his brother's shoulder. "Morning, Liz!"

Sawyer groaned. He should've known better.

"Morning, Holden," she said from the back of the apartment.

"I'll give you both a minute to throw something on, and then I'm coming in. I need to speak with you two."

"Don't tell Mom she's here," Sawyer said.

"Why? She'd love to see her."

One step at a time. Sawyer let out a heavy breath. "Please. If not for me, then for Liz."

Holden gave a one-shoulder shrug, which was noncommittal at best. "Go get dressed, you filthy coyote."

Shaking his head, Sawyer closed the door and went back to the bedroom. Liz was already in the bathroom, brushing her teeth. After running a quick comb through her hair, she threw on clothes. While he waited for her, he got coffee started.

Coming into the living room, she was dressed in trousers and a button-down shirt—sans scarf. He didn't know if she'd leave the apartment without one but was happy to see she didn't feel the need to have it on when speaking with Holden.

Sawyer let his brother in, and he gave Liz a hug and a kiss on the cheek.

"We've got something to share, too." Sawyer grabbed three mugs and set them on the kitchen counter. "Who goes first?"

"Well, if your news has anything to do with that nasty cut on your head and the roadblocks that were set up last night around Bison Ridge, then you're up."

Sawyer poured the coffee and filled his brother in on what happened, as well as the necessity to keep Liz out of harm's way by bringing her to the ranch.

"Wow," Holden said with a grim look. "I'm glad you two are all right. You should've been out here at the ranch all along." He eyed Liz. "Am I supposed to keep this from Mom and Dad? The Liz secret is big enough. And don't expect me to keep it from Grace. My wife and I don't keep secrets from each other. Speaking of which, Grace is going to want to meet you, Liz. I promise you'll love her."

Liz drew in a deep breath. "I'll see everyone before I go back to Virginia." She patted his arm. "I promise."

Sawyer's chest tightened. He didn't know how things would work out yet, but he didn't intend to be separated from her, doing this long distance.

Holden glanced at him, most likely sensing what was on Sawyer's mind. "Well, I stopped by to let you know that Neil Steward and Chuck Parrot are dead."

"What?" Liz gasped. "How?"

"Car bomb with Neil. Same set up as yours, Sawyer. Parrot was different. His house burned down with him inside."

Another gruesome way to go. "Why wasn't I called?" Sawyer asked.

"It was clearly arson. Parrot must have fallen asleep drunk on his sofa. The window in his back door was broken. That's how our perp got in. He poured gasoline around the couch, and based on how severely Parrot's body was burned, we suspect he doused him, too, and then set it on fire."

"That's terrible." Horror soured his stomach. "Are they sure the accelerant was gasoline?"

Holden put a fist on his hip. "Here's the kicker, the guy left the five-gallon plastic gas can behind on the back porch steps. We dusted for fingerprints, but nothing."

Liz held her coffee cup in both hands. "Was Russo able to get anything out of Neil Steward before he was killed? Or Aleida's husband, Mr. Martinez?"

"Neil had nothing new to share. Claimed he got a business loan."

"Same as Parrot," Sawyer said.

"As for Martinez, Aleida told him it was family money that allowed her to invest in Compassionate Hearts franchise and open a store. He told Russo that Aleida was determined to give back to the community and to make a difference. Like a woman on a mission."

"Maybe one of redemption." Sawyer glanced at Liz. She had that faraway look in her eyes. Her wheels were turning. "What are you thinking about?"

"How Holden doesn't keep secrets from his wife," she said, glancing between them. "We need to talk to Evelyn Steward." Liz sipped her coffee. "She was married to Neil for twenty-four years. She must know something, and if she does, with Neil dead, there's no longer any reason for her to protect his secret."

THEY FOUND EVELYN STEWARD coming out of the funeral director's office.

She shook the man's hand. "Thank you for the support and the guidance. For taking care of everything."

"Certainly. That's why we're here."

Liz was never comfortable at funerals. The music, the flowers, the ceremony of endless words and weeping. She recognized it was necessary for closure and to celebrate a deceased person's life. An opportunity not to grieve alone. It simply made her uneasy.

Turning, Evelyn lumbered down the hall, her clothes disheveled, her eyes red-rimmed. Liz and Sawyer approached her.

"Mrs. Steward, I'm Agent Kelley and this is Fire Marshal Powell. We're very sorry for your loss. We know this is a difficult time for you, but we need to speak with you for a moment."

Wringing her hands, the grieving woman nodded.

Sawyer showed her into an empty room where they could speak privately. "Mrs. Steward, we'd like to talk to you about Neil."

Evelyn sank down into a chair and burst into tears. Digging into her purse with a shaky hand, she pulled out a tissue. "First Mikey. Now Neil. I have to organize a double funeral." She sobbed uncontrollably.

Giving her a minute, Liz sat beside her and put a comforting hand on her shoulder. She had no idea what a mother must feel, or a wife, much less someone who had to bury a son and a husband at the same time.

Liz waited for Evelyn to regain her composure. "Did Neil tell you about the threatening phone call he received the night the Cowboy Way was burned down?"

"The night Mikey…" Dabbing at the tears in her puffy eyes, she nodded.

"What did the perpetrator say to Neil?" Sawyer asked.

"Um, the guy told him Neil deserved what was about to happen." Evelyn wiped her nose. "Fireworks. That he was going to take the shop and our son." Her voice quivered.

Liz leaned forward, putting her forearms on her thighs. "Did he tell Neil why he was being punished?" she asked, and Evelyn hesitated. "If you keep Neil's secret and don't tell us what he was hiding, we won't be able to bring the man who did this to justice."

"I told Neil the same thing." More tears swam in her eyes. "That's why he wouldn't let me go with him to the sheriff's office. He thought I might let something slip. By accident or on purpose."

She exchanged a knowing glance with Sawyer. "Let what slip?"

"Neil was being punished for what happened to Timothy." Evelyn took a shuddering breath. "That's what the man said."

"Who's Timothy?" Sawyer asked.

Evelyn shrugged. "I don't know."

Impatience flashed through Liz, but she reminded herself

of what this poor woman must be going through. "You know more than you realize. Your husband must've said something about it. I'm sure you questioned him."

"Questioned him?" She shook her head. "Not at first. We were too busy trying to find Mike, and by then, it was too late. But later, yeah. We got into a horrible fight. He said he couldn't talk about it. To protect me. From legal action. In case I went to the authorities."

"What kind of legal action?" Liz wondered. "Was he worried you would be implicated in a crime and that we might arrest you?"

"No." Tears spilled from her eyes. "He was worried about us getting sued."

Liz looked at Sawyer, and he shared in her confusion.

"We don't understand," he said.

"Neil signed an NDA."

"A nondisclosure agreement?" Liz asked for clarification because it came out of left field.

"Sixteen years ago, Neil up and quit his job at the Wild Horse Ranch. Out of the blue. Something happened. Something bad. He wouldn't talk about it. Because he'd signed an NDA." Her fingers clenched in her lap. "He was worried I might tell my mother. Or my sister. Or my best friend Kim. It's true, it's hard for me to keep secrets. My husband, knowing me so well, never shared the details. But he had a stack of money. Fifty thousand dollars. I'd never seen so much cash in my life. He decided to pursue what he loved. Drawing and ink. Eventually we saved enough and opened the Cowboy Way." Tears welled in her eyes. "We never talked about where the money came from or why it was given to him. Not until he got that phone call. He said he couldn't talk about Timothy because of the NDA. That's when I realized it was tied to whatever happened back then. I pushed him and I screamed at him, demanding to know if he had hurt or killed this Timothy. Needing to understand what was happening to us and why. He swore to me that he wasn't the one who had killed him."

Killed him? "It happened during the summer, sixteen years ago when Neil quit and came home with the money," Liz said.

"Yeah." Evelyn nodded. "Right around the Fourth of July. I remember sitting outside with him, drinking a beer, fanning myself with some of that money while we watched the fireworks."

Fireworks.

Liz combed through her memories, trying to remember any Timothy from the Durbin's. A camper or ranch hand.

Then it came to her. "Thank you, Mrs. Steward. You've been very helpful." She rose and started to move away when Evelyn caught her arm hard and it was all Liz could do not to flinch. She didn't, shaken when the woman's eyes filled with tears.

"Please find the wretched person who did this," Evelyn whispered, then let her go.

Liz straightened, her arm stinging like a live wire had zipped through it. "We will." She handed her one of her cards. "If you need me, call."

"Can you get their bodies released as fast as you can so I can—" her voice broke "—so I can bury them?"

"We'll do everything we can." Liz stalked out of the room with Sawyer beside her and they headed for the parking lot.

"I saw it in your eyes," Sawyer said. "What is it?"

"I remember a camper from that summer. New kid like me. Timothy. But he didn't die."

Chapter Sixteen

"I checked the records, sixteen years ago, around the Fourth of July," Holden said, setting down a folder on the desk. "There is an incident report. No 911 call, but Sheriff Jim Ames was called out. A kid died. Timothy Smith."

Shock washed over Liz's face.

Sawyer opened the folder, setting it where she could look along and read through it.

"I don't understand," Liz said. "A group of us were going out riding. Before we got too far out, I realized my horse had lost a shoe. One of the ranch hands, CP, told me to head back to get it fixed. When the others got back, the group was quiet, uneasy. Someone told me that Timothy had fallen. Broken his leg. But I remember the sheriff showed up and, a while later, an ambulance."

"Right here." Sawyer directed her where to look. "A fatal injury sustained from fireworks. The death was ruled accidental."

"If he died, wouldn't it have been in the news?" she asked.

Holden sighed. "I checked that, too. There was nothing in the paper."

"Whatever happened, they covered it up." Liz pressed a palm to her forehead. "The Durbins paid for silence."

Sawyer glanced at the list of kids and ranch hands who had been interviewed. Albert Goldberg, Chuck Parrot, Courtney

O'Hare, Ermenegilda Martinez, Flynn Hartley, Neil Steward, Randy Tillman, Scott Unger. He got to the last name and clenched his jaw. "I don't think it was the Durbins who paid."

He pointed to the name William Schroeder. "I think Bill's daddy did."

"What I don't get is the sheriff came to the ranch." Liz pushed hair back behind her ear. "How was there a cover up, with people signing NDAs and getting paid off?"

A deep line creased Holden's brow. "You've missed a lot. Sheriff Ames ended up being dirty. You remember Dean and Lucas Delgado from school?"

She nodded. "Yeah, of course. It was because of Dean that Delgado's became the hangout spot."

"They killed Ames." At her surprised look, he continued. "Long story, but they're CIA now."

"Guess I have missed a lot."

"In the fallout of the scandal surrounding Ames, Holden went through a rough patch," Sawyer confided.

Holden shook his head. "Don't bring that up."

"Why was it rough?" she asked.

Holden sighed. "I'll tell her. I was deputy when everyone found out about the sheriff being dirty, and I didn't see the corruption right under my nose. Everybody thought I was either dirty, too, or an incompetent fool. That pretty much sums it up."

Liz reached out, took his hand, and gave it a squeeze. "I'm sorry."

"I got through it."

"My guess is that back then," Sawyer said, "with the Durbins and Schroeders being tight, Dave called Bill's dad and asked him how he wanted to handle the situation. From there, one of them contacted the sheriff, knowing he would go along with a cover-up for the right price."

Her shoulders stiffened. "If Bill's father orchestrated the payouts and the NDAs, then Bill must be responsible for Timothy's death. That would not only make him a target but the biggest one. Maybe our guy blames him the most and is saving him for last."

Holden headed for the door. "I'll get a deputy over to city hall to protect our esteemed mayor."

Picking up the file, Liz sat back in her chair as she looked it over. "Do you know if Roger Norris was the medical examiner at that time?" she asked Sawyer.

"I've been fire marshal longer than he's been ME. You want me to check with him, pull the case and give us his assessment of whether the death was accidental or not?"

"Exactly." She leaned over and gave him a quick kiss before turning her attention back to the file.

Although she had chosen to wear the scarf around her neck, she was lighter, looser, but not any less focused or dedicated. He liked it. A lot.

Sawyer made the call to Roger. Voicemail. Stifling a groan, he left a message and marked it Priority.

"Hey, I noticed something reading the sheriff's report. He wrote that he'd taken ten statements. But there are only nine. They're pretty much all verbatim. Like reading a script."

"Ames could've made a mistake." He got up and stretched his legs. "Or maybe he did take ten statements, but one person wasn't willing to accept the hush money, so they found a different way to silence them."

"Sloppy not to go over the report with a fine-toothed comb to ensure no errors in your counting," she said.

"Well, he was the sheriff, with powerful friends. His arrogance probably made him careless." He touched the cut on his forehead but didn't let Liz see him wince.

"If our guy is doing all of this because of something that

happened sixteen years ago, why now?" she asked. "Why not last year? Why not eleven years ago?"

Unease trickled down his spine as a thought occurred to him. "What if he did try before? Fifteen years ago."

She stiffened. "The fire at the camp that killed the Durbins. It would've been around the anniversary of Timothy's death." Her hand went to her throat. "It would make sense. They never found out who did it. No suspects. But why wait fifteen years to go after everyone else?"

At a loss, Sawyer shrugged. "They all have more to lose now than they did then."

Considering it, she nodded slowly. "We should talk to Timothy's mother. Louise Smith. The father died twenty years ago."

"Then let's."

She sighed. "I prefer to do it face-to-face, but Mrs. Smith lives in Big Piney."

That was a four-hour drive. He picked up the phone. "What's the cell number?" She read it off and he dialed. Once it started ringing, he put it on speaker.

"Hello," an older woman said.

"Hi, is this Mrs. Louise Smith?" he asked.

"Yes, yes, it is."

"My name is Sawyer Powell. I'm a fire marshal with the Laramie Fire Department and I'm here with Special Agent Liz Kelley."

"Are you calling about the recent fires? If so, I don't have any information that could help."

His gaze slid to Liz, and she sat forward with a shrug.

"Mrs. Smith, why would you think we're calling about the recent fires in Laramie?" Liz asked.

"Because that's all anyone in town can talk about."

Sawyer scratched his chin. "In Big Piney?"

Mrs. Smith chuckled. "Why heavens, no. Here in Laramie. I'm in town staying at my mother's place. Well, actually, it's my daughter's now. She got it in the will."

"May we stop by and talk to you in person?" Liz scooted to the edge of her seat. "We had some questions about your son, Timothy. About his death."

"Oh, um, well, I don't see why not." Louise gave them the address.

"Thank you. We're headed over now. See you shortly." Sawyer disconnected and grabbed his hat.

LIZ TOOK THE glass of lemonade Mrs. Smith handed her from the tray. "Thank you."

"Certainly." A petite graying woman in her late fifties, Louise Smith handed one to Sawyer. "I whipped up some sandwiches for you. I didn't have time for anything else. They're made with Wyomatoes."

They looked lovely—little tea sandwiches with the crusts cut off. Liz salivated, thinking about eating one. She loved Wyomatoes. Another thing she missed living in Virginia. The organic tomatoes grown at a high elevation in Big Piney at the Wyomatoes Farm. They had a specific sweetness and juiciness to them unlike any others. But she found it difficult to stomach food when discussing death, and her paranoia didn't allow her to eat anything prepared by a stranger unless it was in a restaurant.

"Thank you." Sawyer grabbed one and took a bite without hesitation. He moaned with delight. "This is delicious."

"Dill is my secret ingredient."

Clearing her throat, Liz set the lemonade down without tasting it and opened her notepad. "As we said on the phone, we wanted to talk to you about Timothy's death. What were you told?"

Louise crossed her legs at the ankle. "The sheriff came by. Told us, me and my daughter Birdie, that there was an accident at the camp. Some kids were horsing around with fireworks. Timothy didn't know what he was doing and hurt himself. Didn't survive the injury."

"Did you have any reason not to believe the story?" Liz asked.

"Kids mess around. Sometimes they do silly, dangerous things. But Birdie didn't buy it for a second. She swore Timothy was being harassed at that camp and that he was killed."

"Did Birdie go to the camp with him?" Liz glanced at Sawyer, who had finished his lemonade and was taking a second sandwich.

Louise shook her head. "I'm afraid not. Wish she had. We were all living in Big Piney at the time. Every summer, the kids would stay here with my mother. One year, my mom thought it best to send him to the camp at the dude ranch. Timothy was a frail boy, sickly, the brainy kind who got along better with animals, horses you know, rather than people. Though, my mom said they had a couple of close friends in town that they met at the local rec center." Louise refilled Sawyer's glass from the pitcher on the table. "Birdie didn't want to go to camp, decided to hang out with her friends instead. My mom cajoled Timothy into going. Birdie said he called her almost every night complaining about the bullying. Mom thought he needed to toughen up. Stick it out. I was torn, thinking it was a good idea for him to be around some men, with his father gone." She sighed. "To this day, Birdie believes he was killed. She's never gotten over it. Blaming herself for not going with him."

Sawyer wiped his mouth with a napkin. "We'd like to speak with her. Is she here?"

"If she isn't working, she's working out. Today is her day

off. I expect she's cycling, running, swimming." Louise laughed. "Anything to lose ten pounds before she gets married. I keep telling her that she's thin enough. It's the curves that she has that got her the man."

Liz gave a polite smile. "What does she do?"

"Health inspector. Good head on her shoulders. Actually uses her biology degree."

"I think that's all for now. Thank you for your time." Liz rose and shook her hand.

Sawyer did likewise before taking another sandwich to go.

"I'll see you to the door," Louise said, rising from her seat.

As they walked through the house, Liz wrote Sawyer's name and number on the back of her card and handed it to Louise. "When your daughter gets home, let her know that we'd like to speak with her. Preferably in person." She noticed Sawyer had stopped and was looking at a picture on the wall. "We're working from the sheriff's office. She can find us there or give us a call."

"Oh, I thought you would be over at the LFD. Aren't you questioning all the firefighters as suspects?"

For someone who lived out of town, Louise Smith was well informed on everything happening in town.

"Mrs. Smith, is this your daughter?" Sawyer pointed to the picture of a woman wearing a cap and gown. Something in his voice raised the hairs on the back of Liz's neck.

"Yes, it is. That's the day Catherine graduated from SWU. Proud day. Happy day."

"Ma'am, if you don't mind me asking, why do you call her Birdie?" Sawyer asked.

"I'm a bird-watcher. When the kids were little, my husband and I would take them all over to the best birding spots. Yellowstone, the Red Desert, Hutton, Seedskadee, Grand Teton, you name it. Back then, Catherine was this delicate, beautiful—she's still beautiful—perfect creature. Like a bird. Been calling her Birdie since she was three. Everyone does. Or used to. When she started college, she preferred it if folks called her Cathy, but I'm her mama, birthed her. I'll call her what I want."

"Please pass our message to your daughter," Sawyer said, his face set in stone. "We have to be going." He took Liz by the elbow and hurried her along to the car.

"What is it? You look like you've seen a ghost."

He rounded the car over to the driver's side and opened the door. "Birdie. Catherine Smith. Is Ted Rapke's fiancée."

Chapter Seventeen

As much as Sawyer disliked it, they had to question Ted in the interrogation room at the sheriff's office. His association with Catherine Smith was too damning.

"He brought a lawyer," Liz said, as though it were an admission of guilt.

Standing beside her in the observation room, he glanced at her. "Only a fool wouldn't have. Our second time speaking with him, he gets summoned to the sheriff's office on the heels of a string of fires and murders. He knows it's not a routine 'let's rule everyone out' chat this time."

She raised a brow. "Why are you so quick to defend him?"

"I'm just not ready to condemn him. He's only known her a short while. Ted didn't start that fire fifteen years ago."

Liz sighed. "Catherine has had friends here for years. It's possible she knew him back then and they've reconnected. The town is small. Catherine spent summers here. It's also possible that the same person who burned down the Wild Horse Ranch isn't the same person exacting revenge now. Catherine could be some siren luring men to do her bidding. All the possibilities need to be examined," she said, and Sawyer heaved out a frustrated breath. She put her hand on his chest. "We need to get to the truth, and you need to be prepared that you may not like it."

He nodded. Unclenched his fingers. "Only the truth and seeing justice served matters." Didn't mean he had to like it.

The door opened and Holden came in. They'd been waiting for him to start the interview since he wanted to observe.

"We can't find Mayor Schroeder," his brother said. "His staff haven't seen him since this morning when he left for a meeting. He was supposed to check out a potential site for an entertainment complex between here and Cheyenne with Kade Carver. They've tried to reach him on his cell." He shook his head. "I've had deputies looking everywhere. They found his vehicle about ten miles outside of town. His phone was in the floorboard of the driver's side."

This horrific nightmare kept escalating. The stakes mounting. What was next? When was it going to end?

Liz eyed Sawyer with a frown. "He was last seen at what time?" she asked Holden.

"Ten a.m. at city hall. He was supposed to meet Carver at ten thirty."

She put a hand on his arm. "Ready?"

With a nod, he said, "Yeah." He'd never had an investigation hit this close to home, pushing so many personal buttons. Something about this case had slithered under his skin, prickling him from the inside out. The sooner they found the perpetrator, regardless of who it was, the better.

They entered the interrogation room and sat across from Ted and his lawyer.

"Why am I here?" Ted asked. He was wearing jeans and a green T-shirt. His black hair looked shorter, as if he'd gotten it cut since they last spoke. "Was there another fire I haven't heard about?"

"Can you tell us where you were this morning between ten and ten-thirty?" Liz started.

"On a run," Ted readily answered, but then he swore.

"Alone. I don't have anyone who can verify it. I slept in at my place, decided to go for a long run on one of the trails through the foothills of Elk Horn range."

"How long were you out there?" Liz asked.

Ted shrugged. "I did a six-miler. Maybe from nine thirty-ish to ten thirty."

With no one to corroborate where he was this morning and his fiancée as his sole alibi for Mike Steward's murder, they needed to explore motive. "When did you meet Catherine Smith?"

His eyes narrowed, his brow creasing. "This again? Why do you keep circling around my relationship? How is it relevant to this case?"

Liz folded her hands on the table. "Please answer the question."

After his lawyer nodded, Ted said, "A year ago at Delgado's. She was inspecting the place and struck up a conversation, started flirting. One thing led to another."

"That's when you started dating," Liz clarified, "but was that your first time ever meeting her?"

Ted straightened. "Um, no, it wasn't. I'd seen her around over the years. During the summers at the rec center. We'd go there to shoot hoops. Play football on the field. Go swimming. Goof off. We knew each other in passing. Why?"

Liz slid a glance at Sawyer before turning her focus back to Ted. "The fires, the murders, are all about getting revenge. For the death of Timothy Smith. Catherine's brother."

His eyes flared wide. Ted looked between Liz and Sawyer in disbelief, which appeared genuine. "Are you sure? I mean, do you have concrete proof that's what all this killing has been about?"

Sawyer nodded. "We do."

"And you think it's me?" Ted asked, pointing a finger at his chest.

Liz leaned forward. "You're a person of interest."

"What did Catherine tell you about her brother?" Sawyer asked.

"Only that he died years ago. That he was killed and his murderer was never punished. I could tell the subject was painful for her, so I never pushed about details."

"Did she seem angry about it?" Sawyer wondered.

"No," Ted said flatly. "It happened a long time ago. Still upsetting, but not enough to turn her into a cold-blooded killer."

"When did you get engaged?" Liz asked.

"About three weeks ago."

"Right after you got engaged to Catherine Smith, the fires and murders started." The statement from Liz hung in the air like a bad smell when she didn't follow it up with a question, only staring at Ted.

The fire chief pulled back his shoulders. "What are you implying? That I burned down businesses and killed people as—what?—some kind of sick, twisted gift to my bride-to-be?" He made a sound of outrage. "I'm no killer, and I certainly wouldn't do it for a woman. I love Cathy. I'd do almost anything for her. *Almost*. I come up short in that area a lot. Ask my ex-wives. That's why I'm about to get married for a third time."

"Stick to answering the questions only," his lawyer said to him. "Don't elaborate. Don't offer anything additional. Understand?"

Ted nodded.

"Let's say it's not you." Sawyer sat back in his chair. "Then it's somebody you know. Someone Catherine knows. Someone who knew her sixteen years ago. Someone who shares her pain and anger. Someone who knows fire. Compassionate Hearts was deliberately turned into an inferno. The restaurant was blown to smithereens. But the cabin was more controlled. Like the one at the Cowboy Way. Help us clear you so we can focus on the real bad guy. The real killer."

As Ted thought about it, his face became stark with tension, and he looked away, causing Sawyer to groan. There was something.

"Ted," Liz softened her voice, "share what you know."

His gaze flashed up at them, his mouth thinning. "I didn't hear a question."

"You thought of someone," Sawyer said, calm and low, hoping to get through to him. "Who?"

"You want me to give you a name and put someone in the seat I'm sitting in right now based on—what?—conjecture," Ted said through gritted teeth. "I won't do that."

Liz's cell phone buzzed. She glanced at the screen. "Would you be willing to let us fingerprint you and administer a polygraph?"

The lawyer whispered in his ear, undoubtedly explaining his options and consequences of each.

Ted nodded. "Sure, fingerprints, DNA, polygraph," he said easily, like a man who wasn't guilty. "I'm willing to do it."

Liz gestured to the hall. Sawyer stepped out with her, and Holden joined them.

She accepted the call. "Kelley." She listened for a moment. "Let me call you right back, Ernie." Liz clicked off. "Forensics are in."

In the office, Liz dialed Ernie and put him on speaker. "You've got me, Fire Marshal Sawyer Powell and Chief Deputy Holden Powell."

"Must be nice to be a Powell in Laramie," Ernie said lightly. "Let's get into the meat, starting with the car bomb. Ammonium nitrate was used. A rudimentary, fairly simple timer with a remote detonator. Small, quite compact. That's where the skill factor comes in. The cap from the gas tank was removed, and the device was inserted there. Moving on to the fires. The marshal's guess was correct. The accelerant used was indeed gasoline. The device consisted of a plastic container, housing the gas with a similar timer but modified to trigger the tool that started the fire. This is where it got intriguing for me and explains why your fires burned so hot. A flare was used each time."

Happy to have his assessment confirmed, Sawyer nodded. "Like I suspected."

"Was it a road flare?" Liz asked.

"Nope," Ernie said. "It was a short fusee that burns at nineteen hundred degrees Fahrenheit. The kind they use in the forestry division."

Liz turned to him in confusion. "They use flares to suppress wildfires?"

"As counterintuitive as it seems, yeah," Sawyer said. "The folks fighting the wildfires are also purposively setting them. Prescribed burns and backfires to starve the fire of natural fuel before it has a chance to break through a certain line. The best defense is a good offense."

"That's all I have for you," Ernie said.

"Thanks. We really appreciate it. Lunch is on me when I get back."

"Lunch for a week."

Liz smiled. "You got it." She disconnected. "We need to speak to Ted again."

Sawyer led the way to the interrogation room. Neither he nor Liz bothered sitting.

He pressed his palms on the table and bent over, staring Ted straight in the eyes. "Forensics came back. Fusees were used to start the fire. It is a firefighter. One who works for the forestry division."

Clenching his jaw, Ted looked sick.

"Give us a name," Liz demanded. "Time is running out. The mayor is missing. This guy blames Bill Schroeder for Timothy's death."

Ted squeezed his eyes shut. Lowered his head as though the truth was unbearable. "I didn't know it was him. I swear it. Right under my nose the whole time." He cursed and pounded a fist on the table. "It's Cathy's best friend. Joshua Burfield. Sometimes I'd wonder if there was something going on between them, maybe they'd dated before, but she swore they hadn't. That they were just friends. But they have a weird bond." He sighed. "Honestly, I think he's in love with her," Ted said, and Sawyer understood why the chief had kept Burfield so close. "Josh has been a wildland firefighter with the forestry division since he was eighteen. A volunteer firefighter at twenty. One of the best—intense, yeah, but dedicated. I didn't know. I swear, I had no idea he was capable of this." Ted looked up at them, eyes filled with anger and disbelief.

"You did the right thing in telling us." Sawyer patted his shoulder and then hurried behind Liz out into the hall. "What was Burfield's alibi for the night of Mike Steward's murder?" he asked Holden.

"His brother, Caleb, confirmed they were together."

Liz shook her head. "This is exactly why I don't trust it when an alibi is a loved one. We need to find him and the brother and bring them both in."

Holden was already moving down the hall. "I'll put out an APB on them," he said over his shoulder.

"We also need search warrants for both their houses," Liz said. "Fast."

Holden gave a dark chuckle. "We'll only need one search warrant. Burfield and his brother live together. Don't worry about fast. The mayor is missing. The judge will hop to it."

Chapter Eighteen

From his usual discreet spot, he spied on Birdie as she finished her laps in the swimming pool at the rec center. The way she glided through the water was beautiful. Such long, clean strokes. Such stamina. He loved watching her do anything. Run. Eat. Sleep.

She was his favorite thing in the whole wide world.

And today, he was finally going to win her heart, take back what was his from Ted Rapke.

She climbed out of the pool, graceful as a swan, water glistening on her skin. Wrapping the towel around her lithe body, she slipped into flip-flops and went to the locker room.

He walked outside to wait for her. Wearing his sunglasses and Stetson, he leaned against his truck. His last gift for her was tucked securely away in the flatbed with the aluminum cover, keeping it a surprise. He imagined what it would be like once she found out how hard he'd worked—the effort, the planning, the sacrifice—to make her happy.

The love nest where he was taking her was prepared. Champagne on ice. After lighting some candles, he'd confess everything. She'd be so grateful, so overwhelmed with emotion that she'd realize how much she loved him. More than anyone else. More than Ted. Because only he would go to such lengths for her.

You're so cool. That's what she'd say to him. *No one loves me like you do.*

Then they'd make love. It'd be like the first time. The only time. After he burned down the Wild Horse Ranch.

This was going to be a *true romance.* One for the storybooks. They'd tell their children about it, omitting a few incriminating details.

The door to the rec center opened and Birdie breezed outside. He smiled, excitement buzzing and crackling like electricity in his veins. He waved and she caught sight of him.

Surprise flittered across her face followed by a bright grin. "Hey, Josh, what are you doing here?" she asked, coming over. "Going for a swim?"

Her inky black hair was wet, her milky white skin damp, and she smelled of chlorine and vanilla.

"I came to get you."

"Me?" She cocked her head to the side. "How did you know I was here?"

"I knew you were off today." He brushed damp strands from her brow, and she pulled away. She did that a lot lately. "Guessed you might be here."

"It's like we have a psychic connection."

No telepathy involved. He always knew where she was, what she was doing, who she was with thanks to the spyware he'd downloaded on her phone.

She was his hobby. His addiction. His love. His world.

"Yep. Psychic connection." He opened the passenger's side door of his truck. "Get in." He offered her his hand to help her up. "I've got a surprise for you."

She glanced around, as if looking for someone or something. "What kind of surprise?"

"The best kind. Trust me, you're going to love it."

"What about my car?" she hiked her thumb over her shoulder at her Jeep.

"We'll come back for it later."

Birdie hesitated, thinking about it, a flicker of something he hated flashed in her eyes. But she took his hand, stepped on the running board and slid inside. He shut the door. Grinning, he ran around, tapped the flatbed, hopped in and pulled off.

She took out her cell phone.

"Who are you calling?" he asked.

"My mom. I don't want her to worry."

No need for nosy Louise to know. He snatched the phone from her fingers and tossed it under his seat.

"Josh. What are you doing? We've talked about this. Boundaries are important."

Boundaries were for the Teds of the world. Not for him. "After the surprise, you can have it back. Come on, you love our games."

They'd played all sorts. The flirting game. The teasing game. The jealousy game, like the one they were playing with Ted, though the fire chief had lasted the longest, made it the furthest. And her favorite—the denial game, where Birdie made a wish for something bad to happen, he'd make it come true, she'd ask if he did it, and he'd deny.

Deep down, she must've known it was him. The denial gave her the luxury to enjoy it without any nasty guilt.

When Birdie didn't respond, he asked. "Trust me?"

Doubt flickered in her eyes again, but she still trusted him. If she didn't, she wouldn't have gotten in the truck. The bond they had was strong.

Unbreakable.

Sixteen years ago, she'd told him her brother, Josh's friend, was being bullied. He'd talked to his manager at the feed store and arranged to make the deliveries at the Wild

Horse so he could check on Tim. Witnessed the harassment and how evil and cruel Bill could be. Even spoke to Dave Durbin about it. The day of Timothy's murder, Josh had been there. He saw the group of them riding off. Timothy, Parrot, Unger, O'Hare, Flores, Goldberg, Tillman, Hartley, Schroeder, Steward and Kelley.

It wasn't until later, after he'd given a statement to the sheriff that had been ignored, after he'd overheard a drunk Parrot and Steward talking about the truth and the payments, that he knew what needed to be done.

He and Birdie had bonded in grief over Tim. Bonded in relishing the horrible deaths of the Durbins and the end of the Wild Horse Ranch. He'd promised Birdie he'd always take care of her, and he had.

"Yeah, I trust you," she finally said. "Where are we going?"

To the love nest. A little cabin he rented outside of town, where she'd be safe. Also, remote, just in case. "Someplace special."

"I hope this isn't anything romantic." The enticing twinkle in her eyes said otherwise. "We've talked about this."

Oh, yes. They'd talked while she flirted and teased—how she enjoyed their games. He was the only friend in the world who understood her pain. The one who made her feel safe. The one she could turn to no matter what. The one who would hold her. But not the one she wanted to have sex with. Not the one she wanted to marry.

Tonight, that would change with a new game. *The love game.* He'd show her she could only count on him, that he was the best man for her—with the greatest, grandest romantic gesture.

He put on a playlist, her current favorites. Once he got her singing, she started to relax. Twenty minutes in, her bare feet rested on the dashboard, and her sundress had slid to her hips, taunting him with the sight of her creamy pale thighs.

The cabin was right down the road, only a minute away when his cell phone rang. He took it out. His brother Caleb. "What's up? I'm almost there."

"No fair you get to use your phone," Birdie snapped, "and I don't."

"What am I supposed to do?" Caleb asked with urgency, which meant something was wrong. "The sheriff is here with two deputy cars. FBI. Fire marshal. They just pulled up. They're getting out of their vehicles. Shoot. Kelley and Powell are eyeing my motorcycle."

No, no, no.

Alarm was a gaping pit in his stomach, but he couldn't panic. Not now. "Grab the lighter fluid from under the sink. Go to my office and burn everything." He didn't want them to know about his big finale. "Then take the spare bike. Try to get here. We'll do plan B."

Caleb disconnected.

Don't lose it. Don't lose your cool in front of Birdie.

"What's happening?" Straightening, she stiffened in her seat. "What's wrong?"

He parked in front of the cabin. "Nothing. A project Caleb is helping me with."

Boom. Boom. Boom. Thudding came from the rear of the truck.

Her brown eyes flaring wide, Birdie spun around in her seat. "Is someone in the flatbed?"

This was not how he wanted things to go. How he wanted to show her proof of his love. He had it all planned out in his head: the champagne, the candles, slowly revealing what he had done. Putting an end to the denial game, because it hadn't served him winning her heart.

Boom. Boom.

Ugh!

"Who is in the flatbed?" Birdie demanded.

Rolling his eyes, he pressed the button on the remote, re-tracting the aluminum cover over the flatbed. "Go see for yourself."

She got out and ran to the back while he reached over, pop-ping the lid of the glove compartment. Quickly, he opened a bottle and saturated a cloth with chloroform.

The door to the flatbed lowered with a clunk. "Josh!" Birdie screamed.

Holding the cloth behind his back, he hopped out and went to the rear of the vehicle.

"It's the mayor! Why is Bill Schroeder tied up and gagged in your truck?"

Wrists zip-tied behind his back, ankles bound, Bill tried to plead for help around the rancid gag Josh had shoved in his mouth. A big red shiny bow had been tied around his neck.

This was not the ta-da moment he had imagined. "I brought him for you," Josh said. "The one who killed Tim. I made the others pay, too, just like you wanted."

"What are you talking about? I never wanted this!"

"You inspected Chuck Parrot's restaurant, getting him on every violation possible. The rating was so bad he had to close and renovate. You told me you wished you could blow his place sky high. Get back at all the liars. All those who sold their soul to the devil named Schroeder."

"Oh my god! That was you?" The horror and fear in her eyes was real, only making his anger burn hotter. Before Ted came along, she would've been grateful. "Josh, you killed all those people?"

Of course he did. He narrowed his eyes. "Who else?"

Birdie's frantic gaze volleyed between him and Bill. "You

burned down the Wild Horse, too, didn't you? I thought you had, loved you for it, even though it was wrong. But you kept denying it."

That was the game.

She wished to see the Durbins dead and the Wild Horse Ranch in ashes. He made it happen. No guilt for Birdie.

She wished for hell to rain down on the others. He made that happen, too. Once again, no guilt for Birdie.

But also no acknowledgment, no appreciation for him.

Did she think she had a fairy godmother of doom waving a magic wand on her behalf?

"I did it because I love you." *I want you. I need you. More than anything.* "You can't marry Ted. He'd never sacrifice for you. He's selfish. There's no way he'd do anything for you the way that I have. This is proof." He gestured with his left hand at the high-and-mighty mayor, keeping his right hand behind his back.

"I love you, but not in that way. I've told you that. You're like a brother to me." She backed away. "Ted was right about you. He said you were obsessed with me."

"That twice-divorced loser wouldn't know what real love looked like if it punched him in the face. I won't let you marry him. He doesn't deserve you. I do. I've put in the work. I've lit the fires. I've shed blood for you. You're mine!"

Birdie whirled, trying to run, but he grabbed her by the hair and shoved the cloth over her mouth and nose. She fought to break free. The struggle didn't last long.

"We'll work this out in Canada," he whispered in her ear, even though she couldn't hear him. "You, me and Caleb." Only a ten-hour drive.

There I'll make her feel right about all this. About me.

He kissed her forehead. Then he picked her up in his arms and carried her inside the cabin. Fishing in his bag, he got the zip tie and bound her wrists. He also grabbed his just-in-case rope. No gag. Nobody would hear her scream out here. He put a blanket on the floor in the bathroom, laid her down gently and, using the rope, tied her bound wrists to the pedestal of the sink. She had enough room to reach the toilet. If she got thirsty, she could get water from the sink. He'd already removed the mirror as a precaution. *Just in case.*

Wiping his brow with the back of his hand, he locked the bathroom door. He'd get rid of Bill in the big finale. Hopefully Ted as well. Every firefighter between Laramie and Bison Ridge would have to respond to the crisis, including the chief, whether on or off duty. Many would die.

With any luck, Ted would be one of them.

Chapter Nineteen

Two deputies shoved a handcuffed Caleb Burfield into the back of a sheriff's cruiser. Liz waited outside while Sawyer finished putting out the fire in the office in the house and started airing it out enough for her to come in soon and take a look. In the meantime, she glanced at the motorcycle that either Josh or Caleb had used in the drive-by when they tried to gun them down.

The radio clipped to Holden's shoulder squawked.

"Chief, you there?" dispatch said, and Liz moved closer to him out on the lawn to hear.

"Go ahead, over."

"The ME got back to us. Norris claims the old report is hogwash. He used harsher language, but you get the gist. Based on the wound, someone else hit Timothy Smith in the chest with a large powerful firecracker. Impossible that it was self-inflicted. Also, a traffic cam on US 30 picked up Joshua Burfield's car traveling north. We enhanced the photo. Burfield was driving. Catherine Smith was sitting in the passenger's seat."

Holden mouthed to Liz, *Are they in it together?*

She shrugged. Entirely possible, but Smith's involvement with Ted Rapke gave her serious doubts. The engagement seemed to be the trigger for Burfield, answering Liz's question about what prompted the murderer to act now. His jealousy and anger were the only things that explained why the fires and murders would coincide with the proposal.

Burfield was afraid of losing her. Must want Catherine for himself.

Was this some grisly romantic gesture? The thought gave Liz goose bumps.

"Does she appear to be under duress?" Holden asked.

"Uh, no. It sort of looks like she's…singing."

"They're close friends," Liz said to Holden. "Best friends. Maybe to her, this is any other day. Business as usual. But we should consider her a suspect as well until we talk to her."

"Roger that," Holden said into the radio. "Deputy Russo and I are going to head up on US 30. Have Deputy Livingston notify the state troopers of the last mile marker where he was spotted. I also want him to track the vehicle as far as he can and check Burfield's recent financial transactions."

"Let the FBI track the financials," Liz said. "We're faster and can go deeper."

"Sounds good. Got that?" Holden asked dispatch.

"Got it."

Holden headed for his sheriff's SUV. "Let Sawyer know," he said, and she nodded. He and Russo climbed in and sped off.

Liz took out her cell, dialed her boss and filled him in. "The suspect is Joshua Burfield. A wildland firefighter with the forestry division and part of the volunteer fire department." She relayed his address and last known whereabouts. "In case Catherine Smith is an accomplice, we should check her financials, too."

"We'll get right on this. Good work. How is everything else going for you?" SAC Cho asked.

"Close call with a car bomb and drive-by shooting, but I'm still standing."

He sighed. "One thing you won't have to worry about is the mayor. I spoke with Schroeder. He got the message you're insulated."

"Speaking of the mayor, he's missing. We believe he's Burfield's next target."

"You've got your hands full out there. If you need any other assistance, don't hesitate to reach out. We're here for you. And Liz, stay safe."

"I'll do my best, sir."

Sawyer came to the doorway of the house and waved her inside. "It's okay for you to come in."

Crossing the threshold, she passed him. "Hope you didn't take in too much smoke."

"I'm good. No worries." He led the way to the office. "You're not going to believe what's in there." He let her step inside first.

On the large wall facing the desk a myriad of photos and notecards had been pinned up. String had been tied to certain pushpins, linking them to others. Caleb had sprayed lighter fluid in a rush, struck a match, and ran. He made it to another motorcycle and had gotten it started, but a deputy tackled him before he took off. The haphazard arcs of fire had burned through entire notes and pictures, leaving others partially intact, a few in their entirety.

Burfield had created a detailed problem-solving flowchart.

Liz went up to a partially burned card that had YER POWELL on it, along with notes beneath Sawyer's name. Then she followed the threads to other cards. "Look at this. He anticipated you being a problem. Saw the Shooting Star Ranch as an impediment to neutralize you. That's why he went with the car bomb. And here." She directed his gaze to what Burfield had considered a subset issue. "He saw Holden as a secondary problem until you were eliminated."

"One problem he didn't anticipate was you." He put a hand on her lower back.

It was warm and comforting. Together they had gotten this far. They had to keep pushing. They were close to getting him.

She stepped back, taking in the full picture, piecing it together. The various problems with multiple solutions, or rather multiple ways, to enact his retribution.

This wasn't a flowchart at all.

"He visually brainstormed murder using a *mind map,*" she said, half to Sawyer and half to herself. Fascinating and creepy, but fascinating, nonetheless. "He's a nonlinear thinker. This type of tool works best for them."

"What if he were linear?"

"For someone who thinks in terms of step-by-step progression, a flowchart works better. Partially destroyed, that's what I thought it was at first."

"What's the difference?"

"With a flowchart, the steps you take to solve a problem are easy and straightforward until you find a logical solution."

"Seeing as how a killing spree isn't logical, I can understand why he'd bypass that one."

She gave him a grim smile. "Now, with the mind map, the center is where he'd start, his main focus and branch out from there." Right in the middle was a card with the remaining letters LL SCHR. "This has always been, ultimately, about getting Bill Schroeder. Everyone else was a lesser piece on the game board to him. Bill's the one he holds responsible for Timothy's death."

"Then his punishment will be worse," Sawyer said. "Look at what's left around Bill's card. One for Ted. And a device."

"He only plans to use one, a single timer, but more complex. Sophisticated. This is different than the others he's used." A tremor of fear raced through her. "To be used where? How?"

"Car bomb isn't good enough for Schroeder. Right? Burfield has taken the more complicated route. It needs to be big for the last one."

"More painful. He didn't just want to kill the others, he wanted to make them suffer. Took away what was important to them. The charity store for Aleida. The restaurant and financial ruin for Parrot. Steward lost his son and shop."

"Schroeder is the mayor, but if he wanted to take out city hall, he wouldn't have kidnapped him. He could've shown up one night while he was working late."

"Bill's reputation and money are everything to him," she said, thinking aloud. "But how could Joshua Burfield take that away from him? And how would it solve his Ted problem?"

Turning, Sawyer looked around the office. "The brother didn't just burn the wall. He tried to burn the desk also. But he was in too much of a rush. Didn't have time to do it right." He went around the desk. Pulling on latex gloves he took from his pocket, he sat down. A cabinet drawer squeaked open. He thumbed through files. "This guy is macabre. He has a folder labeled *Finale*."

Liz came around the desk beside Sawyer as he opened the folder. They riffled through the contents. Page after page of information about the Schroeder Farm and Ranch Enterprises.

"Bill's family holdings are more than one company," she said. "It's way too big and diversified to take out with one device. They have various offshoots in different locations.

Seeds, seed treatments, crop protection, financial services for the smaller farmers, precision agriculture services—"

Sawyer swore. "There might be a way. A horrible way." He fingered through pages quickly, stopping when he found what he wanted. "The fertilizer plant." He pulled out a collage of photos that had been taken of the plant the Schroeders owned.

Liz took a page and scrutinized the angles, what he had zoomed in on. "Burfield took pictures of all the weaknesses. No fenced perimeter. No guardhouse. It doesn't even look like there are cameras on the buildings. How is this possible?"

"Unfortunately, it's more common than you'd realize. This is where he stole the ammonium nitrate that he used for the car bombs."

"How bad are we talking if he sets a fire there?"

"The most recent incident at a fertilizer plant that I can think of was in North Carolina."

"Yeah, I heard about that. The entire town had to be evacuated."

"They had five hundred tons of combustible ammonium nitrate housed at that plant. That's almost more than double was present at the deadly blast in Texas, which killed many, injured hundreds, damaged homes and left a hundred-foot-wide crater. Doesn't he realize or care that most of the people who died there were first responders?"

"I think he's interested in one particular first responder dying—Ted Rapke." All this to get rid of one man and to have one woman? Sickening. "Doesn't OSHA regulate these facilities?" she asked, referring to the Occupational Safety and Health Administration.

"It's complicated." Sawyer homed in on a different page. After poring over it, he handed it to her. "Looks like OSHA didn't put the Schroeder Fertilizer plant on their national emphasis plan that has strict guidelines because it's exempt as a retail facility." He slid another page over to her. "This isn't good. Burfield pulled a copy of the Schroeder's last filing with the EPA."

She picked up the document. "This is public data?"

"Sure is. Do you see it?"

"What exactly am I looking for?"

"Any facility that has more than one ton or four hundred pounds of ammonium nitrate on hand is supposed to report it under federal law. Based on these pictures of the facility that Burfield took, there's close to a thousand tons at the Schroeder plant, but they haven't been reporting it."

"Why wouldn't they report it?"

"Tighter federal scrutiny, additional regulations. To save on expenses."

"At the cost of jeopardizing lives," she said, disgusted.

"If Burfield sets a fire and the plant explodes, it not only destroys the Schroeder reputation and could ruin them financially, but it'll be catastrophic."

"They're going to do it." Liz disconnected from the Laramie Police Department, looking somewhat relieved.

Driving to the Schroeder Fertilizer Plant, Sawyer nodded and swerved around a vehicle, then hit the accelerator. They were on their way to make sure Burfield wasn't at the fertilizer plant and, if he arrived, wouldn't be able to go through with his diabolical plan.

Calling the LPD had been their best option since his brother Holden and the sheriff's office were busy tracking Joshua Burfield, questioning his brother, Caleb, and searching for the mayor.

"They're going to start evacuating the northwest part of

town that would be most impacted in a worst-case scenario," Liz said, "but they think they'll have difficulty getting the residents of the Silver Springs Senior Living and Memory Care Center out. Took longer than I expected to coordinate because the chief of police is on vacation."

"With the sheriff. They're together. Didn't think to mention it."

"Holden's brother-in-law, the sheriff, is engaged to the chief of police?"

"Yeah."

"I take it my mother is aware of that also?"

"She met them both at the wedding."

Liz stiffened.

He put a hand on hers. "She wasn't being disloyal to you. We both love you."

"I guess I'm mostly mad at myself, if I'm being honest. I was in the dark because I wanted it that way." She let out a heavy breath, but her shoulders remained stiff. "Did you have any luck reaching someone at the plant?"

"They closed an hour ago. No one answered. No emergency number was left on the outgoing voicemail."

Pulling up to the Schroeder Fertilizer Plant, Liz pointed out the three-story building with a heavily slanted roof that had been the primary focus of Burfield's surveillance. "It's that one."

They entered the premises, passing several buildings. Sawyer drove across a large dirt lot where big delivery trucks were parked, heading toward the large gray building in the back of the property. Coming around the row of trucks to the front of it, he came to a halt.

A silver truck was parked near the entrance. Same license plate that authorities were looking for. "Burfield is here."

"I'll call it in." Liz whipped out her phone again and notified the LPD. "Get SWAT out here. We have to assume he has Mayor Schroeder and Catherine Smith inside." Irritation crossed her face as she listened. "Fine. But don't send any uniformed officers here. In case this goes wrong, I don't want them getting killed in the blast. Focus on evacuation." She disconnected. "The captain told me it would take SWAT a couple of hours to get here. Why on earth would it take that long?"

"They're coming from Cheyenne. Laramie doesn't have the funding for our own special weapons and tactics team. Not that our community usually has much need for SWAT."

"This is the first time I miss Virginia."

"I'll go in through the front," Sawyer said. "You go around back."

Liz grabbed his arm, stopping him. "Move the vehicle to the side of the building where there are no windows and Burfield can't see it. Then I'll go in through the front. You through the back."

"Why?"

"Who do you think Burfield will see as the bigger threat? You or me? Of course you and Burfield would be wrong," she said, and he tried not to take offense. "Which one of us would be better at getting inside his head?"

He stifled the growl climbing up his throat.

"I'll convince him I'm here alone," she said. "You go in through the back or some other way."

"I can't put you in his crosshairs."

"Half the town is already in his crosshairs. We have to stop him. If you get a shot at him, take it. No matter what."

He didn't wait fifteen years to get her back only to lose again now. "I won't do it if you're in the line of fire."

"This is the job I signed up for. One of us might have to make a tough call in there. Trying to save me won't save the town or ultimately me. If he detonates, we're all dead anyway," she said matter-of-factly.

She was amazing, more incredible than he'd realized, and her logic irrefutable. Nonetheless, his heart protested.

He drove to the side of the building, parked and shut the engine.

Liz turned to get out, but he put a hand on her shoulder, stopping her.

He cupped her face and kissed her on the lips. Quick and hot and sure. "Marry me?" He'd never gotten to ask her, and he wasn't going to let another chance slip by.

She blinked in surprise, her lips parting before her expression turned stony. "I don't want a doomsday proposal. We get through this and you still want marry me, ask again." She jumped out of the vehicle.

Man, he loved her. He jumped out as well. They left the doors open, drew their weapons and went in opposite directions.

In the back, he darted past the large rolling bay doors where trucks would enter to be loaded up and caught sight of exterior stairs that led to the top. On one side of the staircase was a long chute that ran from the third floor to the ground. Another way to load trucks with materials. He scanned the top. A conveyor belt system ran from the chute inside the building. That was his way in.

LIZ WAS ALMOST at the front door when her cell vibrated. She looked at the text message from her boss.

Burfield rented a cabin in Wayward Bluffs. Sheriff's dept found C. Smith tied up inside.
No sign of the mayor.

She slipped the phone back in her pocket.

Taking a deep breath, Liz slowly opened the front door. A slight creak in the hinges announced her presence. Tension twisted in every muscle in her body. She wished Sawyer better luck.

She eased inside, her gun in a two-handed hold. Passing equipment and stacks of empty sacks labeled with the Schroeder name, she inched deeper into the building. She eyed seven massive bins lined up in a row against the back wall and edged around a couple of front-end tractor loaders.

There was an aluminum wall instead of a four-foot thick concrete one per OSHA regulations, with an opening large enough for two tractors to get through simultaneously. Beyond the wall, a large mound of ammonium nitrate sat in the middle of the building.

She crept forward. Her skin crawled. Wherever Burfield was, he knew she was there, and he was watching.

Her heart hammered in her chest as she glanced around. A conveyor belt ran from the top of the building near the ceiling, across its length, down to the heap of chemicals. She eased around the pile of whitish-gray granules. Braced for anything.

Then Bill Schroeder shuffled into view, ankles bound, a red bow around his neck as Burfield hauled him forward, hiding behind the mayor. Lean, with an athletic build, Josh was taller by a couple of inches and had to hunch. Schroeder's terrified eyes met hers, sweat beading his forehead, his skin sickly pale.

Liz raised her weapon, taking aim.

"I wouldn't if I were you." Burfield held up the detonator in his other hand and gestured with his head at the device he'd planted next to the ammonium nitrate. "I'll blow us all to kingdom come right now. Where's Sawyer?"

"Not here."

Burfield laughed. "You expect me to believe that he left you all alone."

This monster saw her as a helpless damsel incapable of holding her own. "We split up. Your truck was captured on cameras on US 30. He's trying to track you down," she said, not wanting him to know they'd found the cabin and Catherine. It might set him off.

His angular face tightened with worry. For a second his concentration slipped, and he let his head edge to the side enough for her to take a shot, but his focus snapped back, and he put his head behind Bill's again.

"Sawyer wanted to keep me safe, thinking you're headed north," she said, "and I didn't want to be a distraction to him. I agreed to make sure the fertilizer plant was secure and that there were no devices hidden while he went to arrest you."

The wariness in his eyes dissipated, but it didn't vanish. "Not sure I believe you, Liz. Maybe Holden is on US 30. And Sawyer is lurking around here."

"Holden is pursuing your brother. Caleb got away on a red motorcycle out back. The entire sheriff's department is after him. The tip on you, on US 30, came in later," she said, studying him. He looked like he might be swallowing her story, but she needed something stronger. "One thing my training did for me was remove the fear of dying. I can come into this facility knowing a twisted man such as yourself, might be inside, prepared to blow the place up with me along with it. Yet here I stand. But what I *am* afraid of more than anything else is something happening to Sawyer. If I know you're here with hundreds of pounds of explosive material, I'm not letting him anywhere near it."

Triumph gleamed in his eyes and a smile tugged at his lips. That did it. He believed her. Now she prayed Sawyer didn't make any noise.

"Glad to get you all to myself. Drop your weapon."

She held her hands up, gun flat against her palm and then set her Glock on the ground.

"Come closer." Doing as he said, she got within two feet of Bill. "Stop," he ordered, and she did. "Any other weapons? Knives?"

She removed the knife from around her ankle, taking it from the sheath, and dropped it on the ground. She dangled cuffs from her finger and let them fall.

"I'm sure you've got more. What else?" he asked.

"Nothing. That's it."

"Am I supposed to take your word for it? Take off your clothes. I need to be certain." His voice was arrogant, almost amused as though this were a game.

She didn't move.

"I don't have all the time in the world and neither do you. As soon as you saw my truck, you called the cops. They're on the way."

"They're all evacuating the town. You've proven how serious you are about vengeance."

"Big, bad FBI agent. You don't need backup?"

Everyone needed backup and she had more than enough. "I don't want innocent cops to die."

"Do it. Take off your clothes. Remember, I'm holding all the cards."

In a way, with the detonator in his hand, he was.

"Now," Burfield ordered.

Liz shrugged off her field jacket and it dropped to the ground. Next, she lost the scarf. She'd done this before when the bomb maker for the extremist group wanted to be sure she wasn't wearing a wire. For some reason, baring her scars to monsters in service of a mission didn't bother her. Slowly, she began to unbutton her shirt.

Sawyer was close. She knew it but didn't dare glance around. Her only concern was him taking a shot if he got an opening.

She tossed her shirt on the ground, leaving only her bra, feeling more naked without her weapon than her top.

"Turn around," he ordered.

Holding her hands up, she did. As she came almost three hundred degrees, she spotted Sawyer inching along in the conveyor belt at the top of the building. But he wasn't at the right angle yet for a good shot. He needed to worm his way another ten feet. Even then, with the height and the awkward position from the conveyor belt, he still might miss.

"You're the only person I've seen up close and personal who's danced with the fire." His gaze raked over her and darkened with intense energy.

"A fire you set." She needed to buy Sawyer time.

"You deserved what you got. I saw you go out riding with this scumbag." He shoved Schroeder to the ground, the man landing with a muffled grunt, and Burfield stepped closer. "You witnessed what happened to Timothy and stayed silent. Did they pay you, too? Not that it matters. Either way, not coming forward makes you culpable."

She shook her head. "I went out riding with them. My horse lost a shoe. Chuck made me turn around and go back to the ranch. I never saw what happened to Tim. They told the rest of us who didn't go out that Tim broke his leg."

"Liar!" His finger slipped off the button on the detonator.

"I would never cover up a murder, much less take hush money. That's not me. I saw how Bill bullied Tim. I confronted him myself, spoke to CP and the Durbins about it." Though it had done little good. "I want to bring Bill to justice."

A wicked laugh rolled from his lips. "Yeah, right."

"I've never liked this man. He's despicable. His family's

money can't influence me. We reviewed the coroner's report on Tim. The current ME says it shows the wound that killed him couldn't have been self-inflicted. He was murdered. The old coroner and sheriff were corrupt."

"He'll claim it was an accident. Same story he tried to tell me. That they were messing around with fireworks. He only wanted to scare Timothy. Didn't mean to kill him. Bill Schroeder will get off."

"Even if Bill claimed it was an accident, he could be charged with manslaughter." She doubted it would stick since Joshua Burfield had killed all the witnesses to the crime. They had no evidence that Schroeder was the one who launched the fireworks, but she needed to talk Josh down. "Evelyn Steward can testify that Neil was paid hush money. And I found the EPA filing for the fertilizer plant. The Schroeders are breaking a federal law by not reporting how much ammonium nitrate they have here. They will see the inside of a jail cell." That was true. "I promise you."

He considered it. For a heartbeat. Maybe two. "No, no." He shook his head. "Men like Bill and his father always find a way to wriggle out of trouble. This," he said, holding up the detonator, "is the only kind of justice I can count on."

A gunshot fired, hitting Burfield in the forearm, and the detonator dropped. Another shot and he staggered backward. Too far back. The pile of ammonium nitrate would block Sawyer's view.

The bullet had struck his shoulder near the collarbone. If the shot didn't put him down, it would make his adrenaline kick in. He glanced at the floor and he went for the detonator.

Liz scooped up her knife from the ground. Adrenaline pumping through her, she raised the blade, driving it up into his chest.

Burfield raised his shocked gaze to her and then fury exploded across his face. "Go to hell."

She backed away from him, Burfield's blood on her hands. "You first."

With a fierce growl, Burfield lunged for her.

Pop! Pop! Sawyer fired a third and fourth shot.

Burfield dropped to his knees, his eyes still with the flatness of death, and fell to the ground.

Liz raced forward and secured the detonator. Kneeling beside Burfield, she checked his pulse to be certain the monster was dead.

She climbed to her feet, put her weapon in the holster and slipped on her shirt. As she went over to Bill Schroeder, she smelled how he had soiled himself. Thinking about what an awful person he was, her dislike for him intensified. She tugged the gag down from his mouth. "Can you breathe?"

"Untie me. I can't believe he was going to kill me. I've got to get out of here."

She stared down at him and considered it. "Zip ties can be tough. Let me go find something to cut through it."

He wiggled around on the ground. "Pull the knife out of that SOB's chest and cut it with that."

"Can't." She shook her head. "It's evidence."

Liz stood and headed for the exit. Bill Schroeder yelled and cursed behind her.

Outside, the sun shone brighter now that Burfield was dead and this ordeal was over.

Sawyer ran up to her, and she fell into his arms. He held her tight, and she squeezed him right back.

"Good shooting in there," she said after a couple minutes.

"Anything for you." He pulled back a little and looked at her. "Where's Bill?"

"On the floor, writhing like the snake that he is. We'll cut him loose soon."

Chuckling, he grasped her chin and tilted her face up to his. "Those were some gutsy moves you made. Risky ones, too."

"Are you going to give me a hard time?"

"Maybe." He kissed her gently. "Definitely. You better get used to it."

"Oh, really. Why is that?"

"Because we're getting married."

She laughed. "First, you have to ask me again. Then I have to say yes."

"Nope." He roped his arms around her waist. "This time I get to make a unilateral decision for both of us."

She laughed harder. Even though they'd had another close call with death, they had survived, and it was time for her to start living.

"Liz Kelley, I have loved you more than half my life. There's no one else in the world who I want to be with. Marry me."

She took a shuddery breath. This was really happening. "My life is in Virginia. Yours is here. And what about your family? You're all so—"

He kissed her, and the reasons why they shouldn't simply evaporated.

"I can be a fire marshal anywhere. Ted and Gareth would be thrilled to get rid of me," he said, and she chuckled. "We can get married at the ranch if you want."

"I'd like that."

"We could take the kids there every summer. We'll have Thanksgiving there with your parents. Maybe Christmases, too. Our folks will spoil them rotten," he said, painting a picture of exactly the life she wanted but had been too afraid to hope for.

"Kids, huh?" she asked, playfully.

"Only if you're still interested in having them."

She'd always wanted to have Sawyer's children. "I definitely want to have a family with you. Someday."

He brushed his lips across hers and kissed her softly. "Where you go, I go from now on. Please marry me so I don't look like a stalker."

She laughed until tears of joy filled her eyes. Her heart glowed in her chest like a bulb, getting brighter and hotter with each breath. "Yes, Sawyer Powell. I'll marry you."

* * * * *

HARLEQUIN
Reader Service

Enjoyed your book?

Try the perfect subscription for Romance readers and get more great books like this delivered right to your door.

See why over 10+ million readers have tried Harlequin Reader Service.

Start with a Free Welcome Collection with free books and a gift—valued over $20.

Choose any series in print or ebook.
See website for details and order today:

TryReaderService.com/subscriptions

RSBPA24R